MY SHADOW IS YOURS

Also by Edoardo Nesi

Story of My People

Infinite Summer

Everything Is Broken Up and Dances:
The Crushing of the Middle Class

Sentimental Economy

MY SHADOW IS YOURS

. . .

Edoardo Nesi

Translated from the Italian by Gregory Conti

Other Press
New York

This book was translated thanks to a grant awarded by the Italian Ministry of
Foreign Affairs and International Cooperation.

Production editor: Yvonne E. Cárdenas
Text designer: Patrice Sheridan
This book was set in Arno Pro by
Alpha Design & Composition of Pittsfield, NH

1 3 5 7 9 10 8 6 4 2

Library of Congress Cataloging-in-Publication Data
Names: Nesi, Edoardo, 1964- author. | Conti, Gregory, 1952- translator.
Title: My shadow is yours / Edoardo Nesi ; translated from the Italian
by Gregory Conti.
Other titles: Mia ombra è tua. English
Description: New York : Other Press, [2023] | Originally published in Italian
as La mia ombra è tua in 2019 by La nave di Teseo editore, Milano.
Identifiers: LCCN 2023007126 | ISBN 9781635420685 (paperback) |
ISBN 9781635420692 (ebook)
Subjects: LCGFT: Novels.
Classification: LCC PQ4874.E728 M5313 2023 |
DDC 853/.914—dc23/eng/20230224
LC record available at https://lccn.loc.gov/2023007126

Angelica

• • •

That world! These days it's all been erased and they've rolled it up like a scroll and put it away somewhere. Yes, and I can touch it with my fingers. But where is it?

Denis Johnson, *Jesus' Son*

The First Time He Saw Me

. . .

THE FIRST TIME he saw me, Vezzosi greeted me with shotgun blasts.

For fear of getting there late I had left the house way early, and it wasn't even nine o'clock yet when I came to a very elegant wrought iron gate, all decorated with ornate figures, in front of which the horrendous mule path I had been following for kilometers came to an end.

Through the ample empty spaces between the decorations, I could see a big lawn and two giant oak trees that cast their shadows over the façade of the bulky box of bare stone that was Vezzosi's house, immersed in absolute stillness. I turned off my motor scooter and tried calling the number they had given me, but no one answered. I took a look around. There was no doorbell, only a chain hanging from a little bronze bell. When I pulled on it, the bell swung back and forth in total silence: there was no clapper.

I was still smiling about that when I heard the loud blasts of three shots and the whiz of the bullets grazing by me. I ran over to a tree and flattened myself against its trunk, my back toward the house, my hammering heart vibrating in my temples.

"This guy's crazy," I told myself in dismay, gasping with fear, as I saw stretching out before me the twisting, dusky mule path, marred by potholes and razor-sharp rocks that I had just rode over to get where I was, the gloomy stand of oak trees where I'd been forced to take refuge, the cliff-like precipice I'd had to ride over, the clearing that had suddenly opened up in front of me, mysteriously, to reveal the desolate hilltop that the hulking house was perched on.

"A raving lunatic," I concluded, and then I turned toward the house again and saw a guy running down the slope of the lawn, with something in hand. Terrorized, I leaped onto my scooter, turned it on, and gave it so much gas that the wheels skidded out from under me on the dirt road and both of us fell to the ground, me and the scooter. I sprang to my feet and was about to run away down the mule path, when I heard my name called:

"Doctor De Vito!"

I turned around. The gate had opened, and about fifty feet away from me there was a Black guy with silver hair, coming toward me. He must have been fifty years old, maybe a little older. When he got close, I saw that his skin was really dark, and there was a shiny little gold ring sticking out of his left earlobe.

"Good morning, Doctor," he said with a little gasp. "I'm Mamadou, we spoke on the phone."

"Oh, yes, sure. Good morning, Mamadou."

I held out my right hand, which he closed briefly in an iron grip.

"Welcome. Go right on up to the house. Don't worry, it's safe."

And he turned on the brightest smile I had ever seen in my life.

It wasn't only the effect of the contrast between his white teeth and his skin; his whole face was smiling: eyes, mouth, cheeks all seemed to melt into a network of wrinkles to compose a portrait of benevolence. It was impossible not to trust someone who smiled like that, and so I smiled back, dusted off my shirt and pants, pulled the scooter upright, turned on the engine, and asked him if he wanted a ride, but he shook his head no.

"No, I don't ride on those things," he answered in perfect Italian, slightly tinged with Florentine, and showed me his iPhone. "Plus, I have to do my ten thousand steps."

As I was going through the gate, I couldn't help but admire the lightness of those thin strips that curled to form flowers and animals, and I had just come to a stop next to the front door of the house, when suddenly more shots rang out: still louder, still closer, incredibly close. I sure don't know anything about rifles, but these weren't the pops of hunting rifles. They were thunderous blasts, and dry, sharp, mean—the shots that are heard in war movies—and they sounded like they were exploding right over my head.

I made a jolt with every blast, and I didn't get down off the bike. I didn't move at all from where I was. I bent over and shut my eyes, and I kept them shut until I heard Mamadou coming toward me, chuckling. As I entered the house, I raised my eyes to look at the stone wall: there was a balcony; it too had a wrought iron railing, right above the door. That was no doubt where he'd fired the last shots from, the *Maestro*.

Mamadou was still chuckling as he led me into a large living room with a glass wall looking out on a veranda in pietra serena, which, in turn, looked out on a splendid view of Florence. I was asking myself how it was possible to see it so well, considering the long road I had traveled to get there, when I heard a voice bellow behind me:

"Zapata, good morning! Welcome!"

It was Vezzosi, coming toward me, all smiles, his hand held out, and the first thought that came to mind was that he was much, much older; the thirty-year-old with the ravenous eyes in the pictures taken in 1995 had turned into a fat guy with a huge chest that spread out in all directions until it blended into his belly, as though over the years his young man's abdominals had grown a bulletproof vest made of flesh.

He was just under six feet, and he had broad shoulders like someone who swam a lot as a kid, a solid neck, strong legs, like a football player's, and long, graying hair, almost down to his shoulders, a little wavy, a little dirty. He was wearing a jeans shirt with mother of pearl buttons that were pulled tight over his belly, light, wide-legged pants with a hole in one knee, and square-toed boots.

Handsome he was not, but he had regular features, especially his nose, perfectly straight, and being overweight flattened out the wrinkles in his wide, vivacious face, in which you could still make out the face of the little boy he had been. Small brown eyes, a high forehead by way of a slightly receding hairline, his shiny white teeth worn by years of grinding played a supporting role to a bright smile that gave the impression of having swept a ton of women off their feet, in the past, before something ugly had happened. Because, looking at Vezzosi, it was easy to see that something ugly had happened to him.

"I see you're not exactly a giant, Zapata. Do you make it to five eight?" he said, squeezing my right hand.

I wasn't prepared, and so I wasn't able to respond to the squeeze, and it hurt a little, too, but I forced myself to smile.

"Almost."

"Good, then you must have a big dick. Good for you. Mine is short, but it's got a nice circumference, and it's still frisky, mighty frisky."

He looked at me in silence for a few seconds. He seemed embarrassed, as though he had finished the lines that had been written for him, and he didn't know what else to say.

"Well," he went on, "now that we've introduced ourselves, Mamadou will show you your room and take you on a little tour of the house and the garden. After lunch you can do whatever you like. Read, write, study, sleep, contemplate, go for a walk, watch a movie, take a shower, or beat off. Whatever you want. This is a place where freedom reigns, and more than that, total anarchy. Not family, nor church, nor country, nor law. I'll see you at dinner. At nine o'clock, sharp. Ciao, Zapata."

"Can we take a picture together?"

My mother had asked me to, a picture of the two of us together. *Take a selfie together.*

"Absolutely not," Mamadou chimed in.

"No, come on, why not? He's got a nice face, this kid."

Vezzosi came over next to me and put an arm on my shoulder, and I suddenly smelled the tenuous, distant perfume of my dad's aftershave, the one whose name was a number. I looked at him and smiled.

"What's up?" he asked.

And me:

"Nothing."

And I snapped the picture.

Day Lilies

· · ·

MY ROOM WAS a lot more spacious than the one I had at home. There was a window with a view of some distant hills, an old wrought iron bed that creaked when I sat on it, a wooden wardrobe, and an armchair upholstered with a flowery fabric.

I went into the bathroom to wash my face, and sent the picture to my mother via WhatsApp, with the comment: *Here we are!*

When I went back in the room, Mamadou was staring at me with a cutting smile. He was a lot older than the fifty years I'd given him at first sight, but he had kept himself in great shape. His body was as tight as violin strings. He was wearing a white shirt with the sleeves rolled up, and the veins in his forearms were popping out like a weight lifter's. If on first glance his shoulders didn't seem that broad, it was only because he had oversized traps emerging from right under the back of the neck and stretching out, bulgy and turgid, to grab on to the shoulder blades, making his shoulders seem narrow even though they were anything but.

"Delete the picture."

"Okay," I said, and I deleted it.

"Did you send it to anyone?"

"No."

"Sure?"

"Yes."

He stared at me for a few seconds. I realized that he was now using the informal *tu*.

"Because the Maestro doesn't want pictures of him going around on the internet and in the newspapers. Understood?"

"Understood."

"He doesn't read newspapers. Doesn't use the internet. Zero. He uses email, but only to write to his daughter."

"I got it."

"Good. So, Emiliano, listen to me," he said, threatening as only muscle-bound old guys know how to be. "Clear rules, enduring friendship. In this house, anarchy rules only for the Maestro. For everyone else, nobody excluded, there are rules. The first rule is: no pictures. You didn't know, so you're excused. But no pictures, got it? Never again."

"Fine."

"The second rule is that the Maestro's quarters are upstairs, and you are never to climb those stairs, for any reason, got it? After what happened with your colleague, I can't make any more exceptions."

"Got it."

"Third rule, the Maestro is writing. All the time. If he goes walking in the garden, he's writing. Even if he's sleeping, he's writing. And he is never to be disturbed. He is never to be spoken to without warning, because he is always lost in his thoughts and he gets scared easily, and he has a delicate heart. He is never to be asked questions. He doesn't like questions. Got it?"

I nodded.

"And now here's the most important rule, Emiliano. We all know why you're here, but there is to be no talk about the new novel. Never. For any reason. Just the mention of it makes his stomach shut."

I nodded.

"He's writing. That's all you need to know, got it?"

I nodded.

"And I don't know anything about it. There's no use asking me. Your colleagues always try. But it's useless, got it?"

Seeing me nod yet again, quiet and attentive and understanding, and even a little bit cowed, Mamadou put away his cutting smile and put his benevolent one back on. I wondered which was his natural smile. Which was the real Mamadou.

"Come with me, I'll show you the hemerocallis."

"The day lilies?"

"No, the *one-day* lilies," said Mamadou, and he took me out to the garden, which actually coincided with the lawn that surrounded the house like a ring and that must have taken an indescribable amount of effort to liberate from the woods, and he showed me some little brightly colored flowers that, he explained, lasted for just one day, from morning to night.

"The Maestro waited three hundred and sixty-four days for them, and he'll wait another three hundred and sixty-four to see them again."

Then he showed me the rest of the garden, pointing out every single plant as though I could appreciate it, me, who couldn't tell a pine tree from a cypress. He showed me the palm trees and the banana trees, and the birds of paradise, and the cycas and the agaves. The oleanders, the rhododendrons, the azaleas, the hydrangeas. The camelias. The hibiscus. The rosemary, the thyme, the sage, the marjoram, the lavender. The helichrysum. The jasmines. The ivy. The passion vines. The wisteria. The bougainvillea. The clematis. The "plumbago or leadwort," he said, he wasn't sure. The strawberry trees. The hawthorns. The olea fragrans. The aucubas. The mimosas. The jacarandas. The junipers. The araucarias.

"They were all planted by the Maestro, personally."

"What is that written on that rock?"

"Nothing."

"But what is it?"

"A sort of target."

"A target for what?"

"For when the Maestro goes shooting."

"Oh, is he a hunter?"

"A hunter? No, certainly not. The Maestro would never shoot at an animal. He says it's bad karma. And besides, he's not a very good shot. He needs a great big target, that doesn't move."

"So he always shoots at that rock?"

"No, sometimes, he shoots into the air."

"And why?"

"He likes to shoot."

We walked over closer to this immense mass that rose up out of the ground at least six feet high and looked like it must have been there from the time of the creation, enormous and immovable, reaching down to the netherworld. I stuck my fist into a cavity in the rock that was right under the inscription MARTA, written by hand in white paint with paint drops all around.

"Marta?"

"His ex-wife."

"And this hole? What did he make it with?"

"A bazooka."

"With what?" I asked him, but he was already on his way toward a small shed, to show me the motorcycles.

"An '81 BMW R80, a '79 Ancillotti Sachs, a '76 Primavera, an '80 PX, an '84 PE, and a, I think, '78 Special 50."

He looked at me like he was expecting some sort of reaction, but I just nodded, and then he took me back to the house, which was a lot different from my idea of a writer's house. It seemed more like the house of some rich guy, or, as my father would say, a *bourgeois*. No empty bottles, full ashtrays, half-naked co-eds asleep on the couches. Not even the shadow of bohemia in those super-clean, all-in-order rooms that we crossed through before coming to the *library*—as Mamadou called it—which, instead, was a large messy living room, jam-packed with books from floor to ceiling.

In addition to the ones cramming the shelves of a big wooden antique bookcase, there were stacks of books everywhere: on top of the leather armchair, on the tables, on the windowsills, on the twin love seats upholstered in red-and-black squares, and even on the floor, in towering piles as tall as a grown man, leaning against the walls. Just how they could possibly remain standing was a mystery.

"You got to be careful how you move, here."

"No, it's all completely stable. Don't be deceived by what might seem to be disorder or even neglect, Emiliano. It's only abundance. As you can see, everything is in order, all catalogued. If you want something by a particular author, tell me and I'll find it for you."

It was an awesome collection. For a lot of writers, it seemed he had the complete bibliography, and most of the works by anglophone writers were in English. On top of one of the piles, I saw the complete works of Epictetus, the Stoic philosopher.

"This is really remarkable. Can I take a look?"

"Well, sure." Smile of satisfaction.

I leafed through it. Some of the pages had ears and underlined phrases. It had everything: the *Discourses*, the *Manual*, the *Fragments*, the *Golden Sayings*. The appendix also had the versions of the *Manual* translated by Poliziano and Leopardi. A real gem.

"Do you mind if I hold on to it for a few days, Mamadou? Sorry to say that the courses I took at the university overlooked Epictetus, and so what I know about him comes from the encyclopedia, but he's a major philosopher."

"Ah, yes, I was introduced to him by Salinger."

I turned to look at him.

"Franny really likes Epictetus," he observed.

"Oh, sure, that's right."

His eyes twinkled.

"Hold on to it for a while, no problem, but remember to put it back exactly where you found it, make sure of it, if not, the Maestro won't be able to find it."

"Thanks a million."

He stared at me for a few seconds.

"And since you're a budding scholar, I'll tell you that there's another library upstairs, but that one I can't show you, unfortunately. It's the Maestro's private library. That's where he keeps the first editions. I shouldn't say this, but there's even a copy of *Du côté de chez Swann* signed by Proust."

He smiled.

"Good for him. But, Mamadou, one thing I'm not is a book thief."

"I know, I know," he said, almost embarrassed, "but I really can't take you up there. I'm sorry."

We left the library and he led me down a hallway with a travertine marble floor into a big room with no windows that he called *the cinema room*, on one wall of which was the biggest television screen I had ever laid eyes on, and in front of the television an orange leather armchair with a small wood table, and on the table a little silver tray, and behind the armchair, wrapping around the room, hundreds of DVDs and Blu-rays and VHSs.

Then we came to the *music room*, whose perimeter walls, around an orange leather armchair, the twin of the other one, and a little wood table, also a twin, with an identical silver tray on top of it, were home to hundreds of vinyl records and piles and piles and piles of audiocassettes crammed around two old turntables and a half dozen voluminous pre-digital tape players rife with knobs, switches, selectors, lights, quadrants, and dials, that Mamadou slid his hand over in a caress as he showed them to me.

We left the music room behind and we were suddenly back in the Apollonian, as though the house were divided into zones whose sovereignty belonged to different people: I visited the kitchen, with its brown and white spic-and-span checkerboard floor and copper pots and pans on the walls, the pantry, with salamis and prosciutto ham hocks hanging to season, a big dining room whose walls were crammed with depressing charcoal drawings all done by the same hand, and then I went down another travertine marble hallway that ended in front of a closed door, beyond which were the *apartments of the*

Maestro's daughter who is studying in London, they, too, impossible to visit.

"The only thing missing is a swimming pool."

"When the Maestro wants to go for a swim, he goes to the beach."

Then Mamadou escorted me to my room and asked me to stay there. At two o'clock he came back with a plate of penne and olive oil and a carafe of water, and said he would come back to get me later. I had the afternoon free, but *for various reasons*, it was better that I not leave my room.

"Nothing to worry about, but it's better that way, believe me."

And so, I spent the rest of the afternoon shut in my room, lying on the bed, doing nothing. As I was fooling around with my phone, I got the idea to google-dive Vezzosi a little deeper, and after a slalom through the dozens of videos of teary-eyed female readers reading long passages from the novel, I dug up a television interview from 1995, in which he explained that he really couldn't explain the success of the book and confessed that he had just given up cocaine for the birth of this daughter. But he was very laid-back about it; it wasn't one of those public purification rituals performed by celebrities to clean up their image. He was smiling. He seemed relieved, happy almost. He made no act of contrition, didn't explain why he had gotten into drugs, didn't put the blame on his success or his family or the cruel world, and he didn't ask anyone's forgiveness. He didn't even say he had made a mistake. He just announced that he had quit, once and for all, and then he said that this would be his last interview because he was never going on television again.

I took a shower, then I sent a message to Allegra to tell her I had become Vezzosi's assistant, and she answered right away, congratulating me. She had read his novel, *The Wolves Inside*. I asked if I could call her, and she fussed a little, but then she gave in.

"Really, you've read it? When?"

"A year ago, I think. Someone recommended it. And it's not bad, you know? Maybe a little melodramatic, no, romantic, but not bad, really. It has a lot of nice bits... He must be a real racehorse, this Vezzosi, because with all the success he's had, he's never written anything else, did you know that? Plus, he's beautiful, one of the best-looking men in Italy."

When I tried to turn the conversation to the two of us, Allegra went back to her usual one-word answers, and after a couple of minutes I said good-bye.

Mama said Vezzosi was *beautiful*, too.

"Wow, look how beautiful he is in the picture; even better than when he was young," she chirped, and when she insisted for the umpteenth time that I ask him to autograph her copy, I lost it. I asked her why he meant so much to her.

"I don't get it, you know? Really, Mama. You're acting like some little girl. And beautiful he's not, let me tell you, believe me. He's fat and old, and all puffed up... He's also rude, if you really want to know!

A few seconds went by and Mama said nothing, taken aback, and I felt bad about having been so blunt. I tried to smooth things over, assuring her that I would get him to sign it that very evening, that book with the dog-eared cover that she had entrusted to me with tears in her eyes, but the damage had already been done, and the phone call ended soon after, miserably.

I had Mama's copy right next to me, on the bedside table. The cover had a black-and-white photo of a boy and girl walking arm in arm in front of the Paradise Door, the door to the Baptistry. I opened it, turned a few pages, read the epigraph.

All the poems have wolves in them.
                        Jim Morrison

"Christ," I mumbled.

They kept me there for hours with nothing to do. While I was playing with the phone, I could hear them talking, laughing, fumbling around, in the house and in the garden, shouting, running up and down the stairs. Then there were more volleys of rifle shots, at least a dozen, followed by an explosion. Scared, I ran to the window and saw a little cloud of white smoke rising slowly from a nearby hillside.

I decided to take refuge in Epictetus, and I practically dove into it. The *Discourses* were so awesome. I didn't stop reading until sunset—my heart buoyed by the words and example of that great master—when Mamadou knocked on my door to invite me to the cocktail hour.

With Highest Honors

. . .

I PUT ON a shirt and my Stan Smiths, took Mama's copy, and followed him out onto the veranda, where Vezzosi was sprawled on a great big wicker lounge chair, looking blubbery as a walrus. They should have seen him now, Mama and Allegra, the most beautiful man in Italy!

He was staring at the sunset and didn't even acknowledge my presence. Next to him was a small wrought iron table with a silver salad bowl filled with ice and a tray, also silver, that hosted two long lines of white powder that certainly had to be cocaine.

Mamadou and I plopped down in the other two wicker loungers and stayed there for a while looking at Florence as it continually changed colors, but I couldn't stop taking quick peeks at the cocaine, which I had never seen in person. When the sun vanished behind the hilltops, Mamadou got up and headed for the kitchen.

"C-plus," he said. And Vezzosi:

"As always, too severe. It was a B."

Mamadou came back carrying a tray with a bottle of gin, three large glasses, some small bottles of tonic, and a plate with five or six slices of lime. He plunged the glasses into the salad bowl and pulled them out again full of ice, dropped in two slices per glass and poured the gin over them, popped the bottles of tonic and poured them slowly.

He served them to us. Vezzosi raised his heavenward, and we drank.

For five minutes nobody said anything. The only sound was our unsynchronized swallowing of icy swigs of those superlative gin and tonics. We were going a little too fast for me, but I didn't want to be left behind, so when Vezzosi polished off his glass and held it out to Mamadou for a refill, I took one last gulp and did the same, even though the ice was making my temples throb.

Mamadou handed us the reloaded glasses and went back into the kitchen. Vezzosi got up, bent over the silver tray, and snorted one of the two lines.

He was very composed, I noticed. No grimaces, popping eyes, or throat clearing like you see actors do when they do drugs in the movies. He snorted it and that was it, then he saw that I was staring at him and gestured that I was welcome to join him. I flushed, shielded myself, thanked him and refused.

Vezzosi went back to his drink.

"Never wear short-sleeved shirts, Zapata. Remember that. And get rid of that friar's beard of yours."

And I thought that this thing of becoming his assistant was already breaking my balls. I hadn't even started yet and I was already fed up with him, his arrogance, his house, his books, his flowers, the motorcycles, the cinema and music rooms, and the library, his frisky dick, his damn sunsets, and even his drugs, and I couldn't wait to tell him to his face.

The whole thing surprised me a little, because I've never been intolerant, and actually I've always had a problem with clashes, conflicts, even differences of opinion—all that testosteronic stuff that has to be argued about and defended by screaming and yelling.

I'd just as soon not try to convince anyone about anything. Anyway, it never changes how things go. They go in the opposite direction from the way I'm going, and so it's no use "getting your bowels in an uproar," as my father would say. Ever since I was a kid I had learned patiently to put up with annoying people, like they taught me to in catechism class, and even with all the practical jokes, ridicule, and insults. Every time the bullies came after me, I took my licks and went home in silence, with no complaints. Complaining was no use anyway. The world is full of shit, we all know that.

But this Vezzosi was the king of the bullies! No, the emperor!

Even before seeing me, he had shot at me, and then he had renamed me Zapata, called me a dwarf and a book thief, left me upstairs twiddling my thumbs all afternoon, offered me heavy drugs and insulted my beard and my short-sleeved shirt that was the only one I had and that my father had given me the day I enrolled at the university and, craven as I am, I had worn today thinking I would make a good impression.

The bastard was trying to intimidate me, the most beautiful man in Italy.

I gulped down another mouthful of ice-cold gin and tonic, stood up, and held out Mama's copy.

"Can I ask you to sign this?"

Vezzosi looked at the book, but he didn't take it.

"Ah, it's a first edition. That's worth a lot of money these days. You want to sell it on the internet like that other colleague of yours?"

"Sell it? No, certainly not."

He took another long swig.

"That's me, the skinny kid in the picture, and she was a Spanish model, who was living in Florence, because in those days, Florence was the center of the fashion industry, with all the designers. She was beautiful, name was Magdalena."

Another swig.

"*The Wolves Inside* is really a dumb title, isn't it?

I shrugged.

"I really couldn't say."

"But the book is yours, isn't it?"

"My mother's. Could you sign it for her? She'd really be pleased."

"What's your mother's name?"

"Franca."

"Franca? What kind of a name is that!"

"It's ready," Mamadou shouted, and Vezzosi got up, stretched his back with a grunt, put the empty glass down on the table, leaned over the silver tray, snorted what was left of the cocaine, and gestured that I should follow him inside.

I watched him walk away and put Mama's copy down on the table. What an asshole, he hadn't even touched it! I forced myself to finish the second gin and tonic in a single, long guzzle. I was furious, and promised myself that he would pay for this, too.

I went into the house, swaying, but nobody noticed because nobody even noticed I was there. They had already sat down at the ends of an enormously long table that could have accommodated twenty or so guests and occupied most of the dining room, whose walls were covered with depressing charcoal drawings, which Vezzosi pointed out to me as he was taking his seat at the head of the table: "All by poor Viani, who was the greatest of all and died in hardship."

I took a seat opposite Mamadou, who, meanwhile, was filling our paunchy wineglasses with a golden yellow wine that Vezzosi proclaimed to be Bourgogne de Coche-Dury. Then he announced that they liked uncooked food, so that on the large silver platters that filled the table were a black rice salad with marinated salmon, a raw tuna belly dressed with olive oil, mandarin oranges, ginger and hot peppercorns, and a carpaccio of thinly sliced Fassona beef with a mince of Pantelleria capers and oregano on which Mamadou had *generously sprinkled oil from the fertile Lucchese countryside, Maldon salt, and Sarawak pepper.*

It was all delicious, really. I had never eaten and drunk as well in my life, and I ate and drank so much that I, slowly but surely, relaxed. It must have been the gin and tonics, I'm sure, and the wine, because the first bottle was emptied in a minute, but while Vezzosi was listing the best and most forbidden things he had eaten in his life and concluding that the best of the best had been *the humble glass eels he had tasted once, as a boy, at the Mokambo in Forte dei Marmi,* my irritation faded and was replaced by a sort of euphoria: I felt like I was holding a loaded gun that I could fire whenever I wanted.

When the right moment came, I would hold forth and tell the Maestro everything I wanted to say to him. I would put him in his place, that big inflated balloon—that atheist, whose house didn't have so much as a single crucifix. I would let him have it, and then I would ride off gloriously on my scooter into the night, drunk and happy.

But not right away. I had to do honor to that marvelous verse of Epictetus that I had just read:

I must die.
If now, I am ready to die.
If in a bit, now I'll dine, because it's time.
Then I'll die.

I would follow the Maestro's advice, certainly. First, I would enjoy those delicacies and that nectar that would surely never come my way again—Mamadou was already filling our glasses with the second bottle of that prodigious wine—and then I would let him have it.

I was so calm, so at peace and in control, that I wasn't even bothered by the aimless story with which Vezzosi insisted on explaining to me his invincible aversion to France which, he said, "I only agree to put aside for wines and women."

It seems that, on their honeymoon, his wife was treated discourteously by a Parisian taxi driver, and that, though not knowing a word of French, neither he nor his wife, they had started to argue out there on the street with this taxi driver, replete with pushing and shoving, and the next morning they went to the airport and left Paris never to return again, not even for the presentation of the French edition of the book, a few years later, and not even for the award ceremony of the Femina Prize, which the book won in a breeze.

He told how he had gone to the airport, looked up at the departure board, saw a direct flight to Los Angeles, bought two tickets in first class, and left for what was, *despite her, a wonderful trip, and also my last with that bitch.*

It was more or less at that point that I realized I wasn't following him very well, maybe because the second bottle of wine whose name I'd already forgotten had gone down the tubes and Mamadou was now pouring the third, but above all because on hearing the name California I became enchanted with thinking about Allegra, who always talked about California and said she wanted to go there to live, and to make a living she would have happily even worked as a waitress her

whole life, because, when she got off work, she would be in Los
Angeles, not in suburban Isolotto, and she could look at the
view from the observatory in Griffith Park, and there would
be a million wonderful things to do, and to do them all would
take up an entire lifetime.

Vezzosi was looking at me and moving his mouth, but I
couldn't understand what he was saying, and so I asked him
to repeat it, and added that I was a bit displeased because it
seemed like one of those scenes in the worst movies, when a
character says something surprising and the person he is talking to understands perfectly, but is so surprised by it that they
don't believe their ears, and so they ask him to repeat it, but I
really hadn't understood what he had said, I assured him, and
that was the only reason I had asked him to repeat, that's all.

"I asked you what you thought of my novel, Zapata," Vezzosi said with a slight smile, as though he had liked my wise-
crack. "How it is seen by someone like you, Sauro Monnanni's
protégé, a future professor and maybe an intrepid intellectual,
but today first of all a brilliant graduate in Classical Letters
who has just completed his stellar university career with highest honors and a thesis worthy of publication that has been
called 'penetrating and lucid...'"

He looked at Mamadou, who nodded gravely.

"... since it even appears that it says something not banal
and maybe indeed new about the relationship between the
Apollonian and the Dionysian in *The Birth of Tragedy* by the
great Friedrich Nietzsche."

It was a stinging blow, and it burned me so much that it seemed to me I had become lucid again, as though my rancor had instantly burned up all the alcohol I had in my body, and had cleansed my mind. He kept looking at me as what looked to me like a malevolent grimace spread over his face, and I suddenly felt hate—that real, pure hate that cannot be confused with any other aversion you might have felt before. *There he is, the enemy*, I said to myself. There he is, the perfect representative of everything I hate in the world. Even worse, the *symbol* of everything that is wrong in the world.

I smiled, took a breath, exhaled, took another big swig of that fantastic wine, and started to speak.

Box!

. . .

"THIS BRILLIANT GRADUATE in Classical Letters owes you the truth, Vezzosi, and, in fact, I'll tell you the truth right now. I haven't read your book, but I don't like it. I don't like it at all. And the explanation of the planetary success it has had can only be found in the shocking small-mindedness of our people and of all of Western civilization."

I belted down some more wine.

"'The last hurrah launched at the peak of the party...the swan song of an aimless generation of drifters, who thought they were so charmed, but who were already enthralled by an incomprehensible, creeping nostalgia.' Poor Monnanni...You know something, Vezzosi? I don't get it, nostalgia I mean. No, I'm disgusted by nostalgia. Maybe it's because I'm twenty-two, or maybe because, like everyone in my generation, I've never lived in a time where I was so well off that I wanted to remember it, but I'm not nostalgic about anything. I can't even afford to be nostalgic. I have to keep on running, in this world of shit that hates me and everybody like me. Nostalgia is a luxury reserved for those of your generation."

I pointed my finger at him.

"What I really don't understand is why you should be nostalgic. Who is better off than you today, eh? You're fucking privileged, damn it! You live your life on holiday, like the man sang, rich as Croesus, served and revered, without anything that could be called a problem, shut up under lock and key in your very own little old world, where you're the master who can give importance to all the bullshit from the past that's not worth anything today. A perfect world in which you can allow yourself anything, even to shoot your assistants with salt, even to keep thousands of books all piled up gloriously in a room to gather dust just because there is somebody who catalogues them and dusts them off for you ... I'd like to know how many of those books you've read, because a lot of them seemed new to me, you know? Brand-new. What is it you're trying to re-create here, the library of Alexandria? Oh, I bet you really enjoy playing the bibliophile. Yeah, because it's not enough for you to accumulate them, you also want to collect them. You want the signed first editions."

Still smiling, Vezzosi launched a glance toward Mamadou, who for a moment lowered his eyes to look at the table, before raising them to glare at me.

"As though books were precious objects in themselves, in a colossal, egregious misunderstanding of their true, unique function, which is to spread knowledge and morality, and in the final analysis, goodness, in a world governed by ignorance and hate. And all of this by way of the grandeur of writing, which, let's be clear about this, finishes with Catullus and Horace, and with Ovid and Seneca, and certainly does not make it to your *The Wolves Inside...*"

I was on a roll. Everything was suddenly crystal clear.

"And all those old movies conserved like treasures in the 'cinema room.' What the hell do you do with those hundreds of cassettes and DVDs and Blu-rays that, I'm sure, you haven't looked at for years? Don't you know that everything is available on the net all the time, whenever you want? What's it do for you to be the owner of a work of art? Didn't they tell you that art belongs to everybody? Unless you... But yes, sure, that's it, just say it... You feel that you're some kind of custodian of lost wisdom, right? The one who keeps the torch burning! It's fantastic, really fantastic! It's incredible! It cracks me up! I bet you even go to the theater every now and then, am I right? And to the opera! Yes, sure, also to the opera, to see those imbeciles with the fake beards singing away..."

They were staring at me in silence.

"And then there's the music. Those *vinyl records* in the *music room*! All those piles of vinyl! Even forty-fives! Because, of course, MP3s are for idiots, right? All that data compression, that unbearable loss of quality... My God, what an abomination! I can just see you, arranging the disc on the turntable, lowering the needle, and sitting there in the dark listening to

Pink Floyd with earphones on and your eyes closed, taking pleasure in every note, because music is a form of art, right?"

I laughed out loud.

Mamadou was staring at me, petrified, and Vezzosi was still sporting that irritating smile of his—but it was fixed, too fixed—and his eyes looked as though they'd been turned off. I had scored a direct hit, but he didn't want me to realize it, and then I swore to myself that I would do it, I would wipe that fucking grin right off his face. I had years of pent-up anger to let out and he would pay for everybody; he had big shoulders anyway.

"After all, you, Vezzosi, are the product of a criminal system. Of an entire century of tragedies and wars and blood and massacres and persecutions and Nazism and Communism and racism and sexism and homophobia and cruelty to animals. Yes, because that's what they taught you, and that's what you taught your daughters and sons, and that is that the world was supposed to be governed by you, the white males, because all the others weren't up to the task, right? They were inferior, starting with the women, who were less intelligent, not as strong, not as brave, and not worth much as workers, anything higher than a secretary they couldn't handle, and so it was better that they stayed home and took care of the children. And the Blacks—or rather, the Negroes, as you like to keep on calling them even now—they were certainly less intelligent, and especially adept for hard labor: they danced well, some of them were good at football, and it bothered you that their cocks were longer than yours, but in their homelands, they had never invented anything, not even the wheel, and so they had to stay in their place... Then, the homosexuals—or rather the *faggots*, as you still want to call them even today—they weren't like you either. Some of them were intelligent, sure, but it was a different intelligence, immoral. Your God, for example, that is, the one that you believe is the God of the Gospels, didn't like them. They were sick. Sick inside. They had taste and style, they dressed well, and they danced well, too, and some were even nice and enjoyable, but you had to be careful because if you got distracted for a second, they took it in their mouths. It was better not to even talk to them and, really, every once in a while you had to keep them in line with kicks and punches, that's how they learned..."

Bitter smiles. They were staring at me in silence. I was going strong.

"Then came the Jews, who were sly and had plenty of money, but they were bad, deceitful, they had murdered Jesus Christ and they were usurers down to the bone. Not in their hearts, because they didn't have hearts! Ah, too bad Hitler didn't finish the job. And Muslims were Bedouins, and all chumps because they still went around on camels and draped their women in veils and didn't eat pork, which is so tasty. Not even the poor were like you; actually they were the worst of all. People with brains the size of walnuts, that you were forced to maintain in the name of Christian charity because they just couldn't make it on their own. And the handicapped?

They should have been locked up in institutions because they were ugly to look at and scared little children."

I took another swig of wine.

"Once you were done with the human race, it was the animals' turn. You felt affection for them, especially for dogs, because they were better than most people and they helped you hunt, but in the end, let's be clear, they were beasts, and they disobeyed, they had to be kicked into line, and in the summer, to avoid taking them on vacation with you, you abandoned them on the highways, and it was 'Off to the sea! Let's go!' Cats, on the other hand, were odious, and you could tie them by the neck to your scooter and drive away, so you could look back and see how fast they could run. Then there was the filth, the garbage. That you really didn't like, but you said that producing and consuming necessarily created waste and pollution and so what you had to do was keep it at a distance or bury it, or in any case keep it away from your houses, where it couldn't be seen or smelled, and so, step by step, day after day, you destroyed our fucking planet, damn it! You filled the oceans with plastic and you also piled up debts as high as your asshole, and now you want us to pay off your debts! You're amazing! Really! You invented globalization and the free market, and you told us they were the future, and then your future left millions of us out of work. You are fucking absolute evil, damn it, you fifty-year-olds! You've pushed God aside and you've taken everything away from us! You have consumed everything you could possibly consume, and left us in shit up to our necks, and now you want to tell us how to live? Go fuck yourselves! We don't want anything from you, and you're in no position to teach us anything! I reject your whole damn culture. Do you get that? Lock, stock, and barrel!"

I had to take a break. I was out of breath. Vezzosi's smile, though rather tense, had held up. I suddenly wondered if I'd be able to wipe it off his face, because I had already taken my best shots.

"You've got nothing to smile about, Vezzosi," I started back up, furious. "Because you are one of the symbols of this tragedy. Yeah, I mean you, who have yourself called 'Maestro' by your... well, yeah, by your Black servant, which is the most racist thing I've seen in my life. 'Maestro' of what? You might as well just have him call you 'Bwana.'"

Mamadou leaped to his feet, but Vezzosi gave him a sign.

"Let him finish," he said. "He still hasn't finished."

"Right, good for you, that's right. I still haven't finished."

But actually, yes, I thought I had finished, but I started right back up so he wouldn't notice, even if I didn't know what else to say.

"But, who are you, anyway? Have you ever thought about it?"

I paused and something else came to mind.

"Tell me, Vezzosi, aren't you even a little bit ashamed to be rich and adored just because you've written a novel, only one novel, almost twenty-five years ago? Don't you realize you've escaped by a miracle, or let's say by a supreme and unmatchable stroke of luck, from all the disruptions of the world, just like that half-blind old codger from the cartoons, what was his name? Mr. Magoo...Shit, while all around you everything was changing a thousand times and wars were breaking out and people dying and nations falling apart and being reassembled, and the poor were multiplying like rabbits, what did you do? I'll tell you what you did. You did nothing. You squirreled yourself away here in this stone box on top of a hill, eating tuna bellies and mandarin oranges and drinking Bourgogne wine and snorting cocaine while your little book kept on selling like hotcakes to airheads all over Italy and all over the world, and you kept on raking in the money, shit!"

Yes, I actually said "airheads." And Vezzosi kept on smiling, but he leaned against the back of the armchair. Body language! He wanted to distance himself from me and what I was saying. *This time I got you, you son of a bitch!*

"You held your peace. For years. Even when they started migrating from Africa and Italians watched them come off the ships wrapped in that gold foil and got scared and discovered they were racists and started voting for parties that wanted to throw them all back in the water, those poor bastards. Not even then did you feel the need to waste even a crumb of solidarity for those desperados, to say one word to your readers, your millions of readers. Not even to the high school kids who go to the beach with your book in their suitcase because their teachers told them to read it over summer vacation. Never, never even once. Not even to say that you were a little disappointed that dozens of them had died drowning, Africans like your Mamadou, and that they had become food for fucking sea bass that you then eat raw with mandarin oranges. You didn't get involved. Didn't let it disturb you one little bit. Bravo! No kidding."

And I started to applaud. In the silence of that room erupted the applause of a giant.

"And there's one other thing, Vezzosi. Maybe the most important. How in the world can you wake up in the morning and still call yourself a writer, if you haven't written a word in twenty-five years?"

"Now I'm going to punch him out, this imbecile," said Mamadou, and he got up to come around the table, but once again Vezzosi gave him the sign to hold off.

"Wait, he's almost finished..."

"Fine, yes, that's right, Mamadou. Wait... because now I'm going to say how he does it... A writer, Vezzosi, you are not and never have been, and you know that damn well. Tell the truth. All you did was have the world's most incredible stroke of luck."

His smile grew broader.

"And now I'm going to demonstrate it... Isn't it true that before *The Wolves Inside*, which, by the way, really is a dumbass title, you hadn't written anything, not even a short story?"

Vezzosi nodded.

"You had never even done a translation?"

Vezzosi shook his head.

"I read on Wikipedia that you never even graduated from university! You got a high school diploma, *Maestro*! And then you majored in Political Science, but things didn't go well, and after a couple of exams, you threw in the towel and started writing the novel. True or not?"

He nodded.

"And is it true or not that you sent the manuscript to Passini by mail, without a cover letter, although you didn't even know him?"

He nodded.

"And is it true or not that Passini read it by chance, selecting it from the truckloads of manuscripts he receives every day only because the title made him curious, and on reading it he was enthusiastic and thought it was perfect as it was, so that not even one word was changed or a comma deleted, and he published it almost immediately, lickety-split, and then it went the way it did, eh? True or not true?"

He nodded.

"Pure fucking luck. Shit," I said, exhausted, and I stopped looking at that smile that wouldn't turn off and that by now would never turn off. I poured what was left of the third bottle into my glass and gulped it down, while Mamadou glared at me enraged. Vezzosi, instead, just stared at me and, incredibly, seemed to be showing admiration.

"Fuck, you're perfect!"

"What?"

My phone started vibrating. I grabbed it.

"It's Passini. He'll want to know about the novel."

"Give me the phone," Vezzosi said, and I handed it over.

"Hi, Passini, I've got to tell you well-done, because you've finally sent me someone with balls. Yes, I'm very happy. I'll keep him. Sure, he's staying on. Yes, sure. Now I'm going to take him to Mamadou's party, too. Good-bye, talk soon. Yes. Very soon. Bye."

And he hung up.

"What?" I said. "Where are we going?"

They jumped up, and I started because for a second I thought they were about to jump on me, but Vezzosi smiled and signaled for me to follow him, and from that moment on everything got totally confused.

"Excuse me, where are we going?" I repeated.

My head was spinning, and they had to hold me up to get me out of the house. We climbed into an off-road vehicle with no roof and all the stars were out. Mamadou drove and I lay down in the back seat and went on talking, but I no longer remember about what, only that it all seemed perfectly right to me and well said.

We clambered down the mule path, and after a bit I begged them to let me out and vomited my guts out, and then I fell asleep or fainted, I don't know which, but I woke up again when we came to a large unpaved parking lot that was lit up like daytime. We went up some dark stairs and went into a place with deafening music and strobe lights where there were naked dancing girls wrapped around steel poles and some

terrible tattooed types lined up to greet Mamadou and Vezzosi, who introduced me to everyone as Zapata, and then he
took me into a room where there was a non-Italian girl, very
beautiful and half-naked, tiny, with black bangs, whom he told
to take care of me, and left me alone with her. She started rub-
bing up against me and I had never seen such a beautiful girl
in all my life, and then I wanted to kiss her but she didn't want
me to because, she said, *a kiss is too important*, and she took
my hand and put it between her legs and I tried to tell her that
I couldn't because I was very religious and very in love with
someone else, but she answered that she was very religious,
too, and very in love with someone else, and then she told
me to be quiet and I obeyed as she whispered in my ear the
words to the sad song blaring out with the volume pumped
up to the max that seemed to me was saying something about
a total eclipse of the heart, and then she sat down on me and
started dry humping me, back and forth, pushing hard, and
then she wrapped her arms around me and went rigid and let
out a moan and came, after which I came too, in my pants, and
she lay there on top of me motionless, all soft, as though she
suddenly had no bones or muscles, and I didn't say anything
because I didn't want to bother her and I started caressing her
back and cuddling her and some time went by and she didn't
move and lay there still, breathing slowly, and then I noticed
that she had fallen asleep. In all of that clamorous chaos, while
the great voice of that woman went on singing about the total
eclipse of the heart, she lay there flat on top of me and I didn't

say a thing and I didn't move either and lay there caressing her back, and she didn't wake up until the song ended and another one came on that was also slow and sad and booming to the max. She yawned, blushed, and apologized, said she was dead tired, gave me a kiss on the forehead and stood up and started to put her clothes back on, that is, she slipped into some transparent platform heels and a string thong that I didn't remember she had taken off, and confessed that she had to leave right away *because in five minutes I've got the lesbo show with a porno star*, and when I asked her how such a thing was possible, she flashed me a timid smile and slinked out of the tiny room while the singer went on about the *victims we know so well*.

When I got out of the closet, Mamadou was sitting barechested on a couch, a cigar in his mouth, surrounded by a bunch of half-naked girls, who when they saw me applauded and cheered *Zapata! Zapata!* and offered me some vodka and I foolishly drank it, and from then on it was darkness. All I remember is that at some point someone said the police were there and Vezzosi came out of a small room, he too with a cigar in his mouth, and there was a lot of commotion and everybody was running away, and I fell down on the ground and Mamadou pulled me up and carried me on his back like I was a carpet, and we left through an emergency exit and while they were running toward the car, Vezzosi couldn't stop laughing, and Mamadou said he was going to remember that night forever, no doubt about it.

Cocoons

. . .

MY NAME IS Emiliano De Vito, not Zapata, and I was born in Florence three years before 2000.

Ever since I was a baby my father always told me to follow my dreams and, when I left middle school, I, who didn't have any dreams, chose the school that he would have chosen if he hadn't had to study bookkeeping: classical high school.

I lived for five years in a cocoon, happy and content to spend my days racking my brain over the classics together with Allegra, the gray-eyed girl who sat next to me and who, by virtue of repeatedly reading Catullus next to me, ended up giving in to my awkward entreaties to become my first girlfriend:

> Let us enjoy life, my Lesbia, and let us love
> And the murmuring of the snide old men let us consider it
> Not worth a plug nickel
> The dying days may come back again

But if this brief light of ours should die,
We will sleep a single endless night
Give me a thousand kisses and then another hundred
Give me another thousand and another hundred,
again, again a thousand and yet another hundred
to trick them all we'll confuse the count,
so that no one can wish us ill
for all the kisses we have shared

Having graduated from high school with highest honors, I went looking for another cocoon. Liberal arts seemed to be the most promising, and I was greatly encouraged by the lofty presentation of the curriculum that I had read on the university website, which promised that I would "acquire a significant knowledge of texts, authors, and schools of thought, as well as the essential elements of Philology, Linguistics, Literary Theory, and History," and that, upon graduation, I would be able to "employ these acquisitions in a wide range of professional pursuits as well as to apply them in completing a further course of graduate studies that would open the way to participation in the recruitment competitions for secondary school teachers or to a university career."

Practically speaking, I had explained enthusiastically to Allegra, I would be able to live my whole life in a cocoon, and she with me, by my side, learning what we would later teach to our younger brothers and sisters, who, like us, were enamored of classical studies!

Her considered response was to dump me.

It was Saturday night, the beer hall was boisterously loud, and Allegra, with a frail, uncertain voice that I had never heard from her, said she didn't agree at all with the story of the new cocoon because she didn't want to live her whole life in a cocoon, no, *but in the world*, and she had been thinking about the future for a while but had only now found the courage—*No*, she corrected herself, straightening her shoulders and getting back her firm voice, *not the courage, I've got the courage, the way and the opportunity*—to tell me that she wanted to take another road, *there, in every sense of the word*, and, in other words, she had to leave me, Catullus or no Catullus, and then she pounded her fist on the table in one of her gestures of ferocity that I loved so much, got up and walked out, leaving me there alone in that beer hall, in front of a plate of cold French fries.

So then I went to take refuge in the biggest and most distant cocoon I could find—Classical Letters, in Rome—and spent those three endless years studying, going to Mass in all the churches of the Holy City, writing her and calling her often and in vain, comforted only by the example of my friend Catullus, who knew my pain and suffering well and who, like me, alternated between hanging in...

Poor Catullus, enough with illusions
and what you see lost, consider it lost.
A blazing flame of joy were your days
when you ran where she, your kindred spirit, bid you

loved as she was as no one else will be;
all of love's games that you desired
were born then and she did not deny you.
A blazing flame of joy those days
Now, she wants you no more: and you, courage, want not
do not chase her like a wretch, if she flees,
but resist with all your willpower, do not concede.
Farewell, my love. Catullus shall not yield,
he'll not come looking for you, he'll not come to you for
     certain:
but you will suffer for not being desired.
Look at yourself, then, what can life give you?
Who will want you? Find you beautiful? Whom will you
     love?
By whom will you be loved? And whom will you kiss?
Whose lips will you bite?
But you, Catullus, resist, do not concede.

and desperation

If there is pity in you, gods, if on death's door,
in the extreme hour, you should ever aid someone
look at my unhappiness, if I have lived honestly
tear me away from this pain that consumes me,
that, creeping into the deepest part of me
like some stealthy torpor, has erased all the joy from my
     heart.

I ask no more that you requite my love,
nor the impossible, that you should remain faithful:
I only want to heal and forget this pain
O gods, in exchange for my devotion, grant me this.

A few weeks after my return from Rome, holding in my hand a diploma attained with highest honors and crowned by the designation "worthy of publication," my father passed away.

He was taken by a sudden heart attack while he was driving, in traffic, at 7:30 in the morning, on his way to the mechanic's where he still kept the books, even though he was retired, and I lost my head.

I mean that literally.

I was totally out of it. Couldn't concentrate on anything whatsoever. I spent entire afternoons taking long walks around the city, taking pictures of clouds, watching television. Sleeping. I couldn't even manage to cry, because I never thought about him. I didn't look at his pictures, the videos of the birthdays and Christmases that we had celebrated together. I didn't listen again to his messages on my telephone. Nothing.

It was as though, by dying, my father had disappeared not only from my life but also from my memory, and so I started to prepare for the collapse, because—as everyone kept telling me—*this is not normal and it cannot last*. Even Allegra, who was busy preparing for her toughest exams in law school and who, because of my pain, had drawn a bit closer, called me.

"Prepare yourself, Emiliano, because the blow will come all at once, and then it gets really rough…"

But I didn't feel anything, for months and months, and in the end, one day that I had gone to the cemetery to take him a bunch of African daisies, as I was looking at the picture of him smiling, I got it.

Sure, the blow had hit me.

It had hit me right away.

This was it, and it consisted in forgetting him.

In losing even my memory of him and, as a consequence, a big part of myself. In the condemnation to remain crippled for the rest of my life, and in need of everything because, now even I had figured it out, I wasn't good at living the way other people did, and my father had realized that ever since I was in middle school.

That's why he had always advised me to take refuge in cocoons.

Because on the outside I wouldn't have survived.

Instead of finishing me off, once and for good, this certainty pushed me to stick my head out again. I had decided that I couldn't force my mother, also retired, to maintain me during the two years of the master's program that I had chosen with my father—by far my most ambitious and illustrious cocoon, the one which, with a little bit of luck, I would never have to leave: Philology, Literature, and History of Antiquity—and I had started looking for a job, only to discover that my three-year degree in Classical Letters was worthless.

The "wide range of employment options" that were indicated as possible in the presentation of my major—and that is
"the professional opportunities in the culture and publication
industry, with responsibilities for editing and textual revision,
the duties of press officer, public relations expert, the drafting
of educational and promotional materials for cultural institutions, foundations, or government agencies"—had vanished.
Some had been suppressed, some entrusted to computers, and
the rest devolved to the activities and capabilities of the Om-
nipotent Citizen, the new fainthearted unemployed sovereign
of the world that had been handed down to us.

It seemed that all those people who kept telling me I was
wasting my time translating from ancient Greek and Latin
were actually right, after all, and that I would have been a
thousand times better off if, *with the brain I had been given,*
I had gone for a nice solid degree, one of those that lands
you a job right away, like engineering, computer science, or
economics.

At every job interview, though, I found myself surrounded
by phalanxes of graduates in engineering, computer science,
and economics grumbling the whole time about savage de-
localizations (some of them said "dislocations") and rigged
hiring processes and nepotism, and cursing about the time
that—in their words—they had wasted attending those
bone-dry, tedious courses and going on and on compliment-
ing me on having had the balls to follow my dreams and study
what I liked, seeing as, in Italy, there was no work for anyone,

assuming you didn't want to be a waiter, and I sure as hell don't want to be a waiter, damn it!

I didn't tell my mother that in Italy there was no work for anyone. I didn't want to demoralize her, plus she could figure it out on her own. I told her that I was looking, and there was nothing to worry about because I was sure to find something.

My English was good, very good, but there were a hundred thousand others whose English was good, and actually it seemed that Google Translate was better than all of us.

Every once in a while, I did some tutoring in Greek. I only had two students, a freckle-faced boy and girl, distant relatives who shared a common stupidity, and who came to my house together and left me with thirty euros in hand; the only money that entered my pocket, because, from my mother, due to my ill-conceived pride that instead of bringing her relief made her sad, I stubbornly refused to accept anything.

In the end, after several more months of humiliating and fruitless searching, I had quit looking. Maybe it was true that there was no more need in Italy for me and those like me—and not only for graduates in Classical Letters, but for anyone between the ages of twenty and thirty. Maybe the only thing to do was to leave, escape, emigrate, look for work abroad. Be a barista in London, teach Italian in Berlin, shelve boxes in a warehouse in Paris? Stumble around Barcelona with your eyes staring straight ahead, looking for traces of Gaudí on the walls of buildings? Pine away, longing for sunlight, in frozen Scandinavia? Or somewhere else even farther away? And doing what?

I spent my mornings at the library, reading, and the afternoons walking around Florence, telephone in hand, posting pictures on Instagram and watching and rewatching American gangster movies and TV series on the Neapolitan *camorra*, and meanwhile I kept on telling myself that that ocean of wasted time wasn't really wasted, that I had to know how to wait, and that even from this endless waiting I was still learning something, and that surely, sooner or later, I would find work.

I warmed my spirits by the fire of the thought that I still had the Greek lessons and that they would go on for months, because the freckle-faces were dolts and, yes, they were improving, but very slowly, and at the end of the school year I could try sticking some announcements on the bulletin boards of the classical high schools to make myself a little publicity and find some slow learners to help over the summer.

Every morning, though, I woke up to see that it was still dark outside and feel my heart beating wildly, and there opened up in front of me another of those endless days, each one the same as the last, impossible to fill, and I got disheartened and told myself that at twenty-two I was already a failure dependent on the survivor's pension of a father who had generated me too late and died too early.

Life had waited patiently for me to finish having my fun time with the Ancients, but in the end, it had managed to grab me by the scruff of my neck, and then it started shaking.

Where Does Good News Come From? From What Far-Off Star?

•   •   •

ON ONE OF the worst of those days, I had gone to see the professor who had supervised my senior thesis, Sauro Monnanni, a brilliant guy, tall and thin, very distinguished, who, up until a short time before then, had been a full professor in Rome, and who dressed with excellent taste and spoke floridly, even more than me.

The door to his office was closed, and so I sat down in the hallway to wait for him, beneath a shimmering fluorescent light. I could hear him talking on the phone, but because of his low voice and the noise made by students migrating between classrooms, I could only hear a few words here and there. Then, all of a sudden, I heard him slam the receiver down and shout:

"Dickhead! Dickhead! You are an enormous, immense, cyclopic, titanic dickhead!"

He jerked the door open and on seeing me sitting there in the hall, he drew back for a second, as though he didn't recognize me. He seemed distracted, almost upset. All ruffled, a scruffy, unshaved chin, he sure didn't look like the Monnanni I knew, the only professor capable of citing during the same lesson Telamonian Ajax and Roberto Benigni, Brigitte Bardot and Guicciardini. After struggling to hint at a smile he told me to come into his office and asked me how my "entrance into the savage world of nonacademic work" was going.

And I let it all out. I drowned him in all of my disappointments and humiliations, big and small, in slogging around searching for work in vain: the endless hours in waiting rooms, the shame of having to ask, the tight smiles of the personnel directors who couldn't wait to mangle someone who had studied the classics, the universal rudeness that rules the world, the dismissiveness of *We'll let you know by email* and then no email actually being sent, the *If instead of Greek you knew Mandarin we'd hire you right away*, the *We're sorry but you are not qualified for the position we need to fill*, the *We're sorry but you're overqualified for the position we need to fill*, until I got a lump in my throat and had to stop talking.

Elbows on the desk, his hands closed in fists holding up his chin, Monnanni was staring at me. Lanky as he was, and hunched over in that position, he looked like a question mark.

"Maybe I can help you, Emiliano."

"Really, Professor?"

"Maybe, just maybe, I have a job for you."

"A job? Seriously?"

"You have certainly heard of Vittorio Vezzosi."

"But isn't he dead?"

A bitter smile spread across his face.

"Dead? No, my young friend, weeds never die. Vezzosi is alive and well. He lives in the country, *not so far from Fiorenza as to be in the boondocks, and not so close as to have to put up with its revolting stench*, is how he put it the last time I saw him. He lives alone, the Superior Being. He cannot stand the company of mere mortals. Like a hermit or a monk, he has been wallowing now for a quarter of a century in a triumphant and self-inflicted and embittered reclusion that dates from the time immediately following the planetary success of his first and, for now, only work, which you certainly know and, I am sure, appreciate."

I answered, yes, certainly.

I didn't feel like telling him that, having chosen the classical curriculum, I had only taken one course in contemporary literature and that it only went up to as far as Tasso, and that I had gone only a little farther on my own because, with everything I had to study, I certainly couldn't waste time with the autobiographical novelettes of modern Italian writers. Sure, I had read quickly those three or four books that you read as a kid and that seem fundamental because, in a word, you're a kid, but when you read them again at university you feel like throwing them into the fire, things like *Siddhartha* and all that other bullshit, and naturally I had read with trepidation

Salinger and some of the Russians—Tolstoy, and Gogol, mostly, because Dostoyevsky I was saving for later, except for *White Nights*, which Allegra and I had loved commenting on page after page, in the good times—but, anyway, no, I didn't tell him that I hadn't read it, that little book that had come out two years before I was born and that everybody had read, including my parents, and that over the years had been recommended to me over and over, and by so many different people, that just hearing the title got my shorts in a twist.

Monnanni was looking out the window, engrossed.

"It's still one of those perfect little novels, one of those gifts from the gods. One of the few works that manage to reveal the absurd, splendid unfolding of life. After more than five years since the last time I'd looked at it, just last night I sat down to reread it, and once again it felt fresh, exhilarating, yet overflowing with a pain that is so human and so pure. But, along with that pain, on the other hand, the blinding light of hope that shines in each of the characters like a huge, benevolent photoelectric cell, illuminating, night and day, their poor, desperate dreams."

He sighed.

"It's the last hurrah, launched at the peak of the party. The swan song of an aimless generation of drifters who thought they were so charmed, but who were already enthralled by an incomprehensible, creeping nostalgia, the portent of an unimaginable future of dispossession and destruction...who are really us, all of us who brutishly follow our days on this planet that goes on spinning endlessly in star-filled space, as Dylan Thomas said, I think. If you think about it, even the title was perfect. *The Wolves Inside*. It could be the title of a song by Loredana Bertè or Patti Smith, yet it touches us all. And if you think about it, it has almost no plot, if not the most elementary: an unhappy love story like we've all had, as kids."

"It was a big hit, wasn't it, Professor?

"Incredible. An incredible success for a book that was first released in a thousand copies, by a small publishing house, without any promotion. Something unimaginable, miraculous, was set on fire. People who were readers, and in those days, they were legion, decided that it was the first book in decades that had been written for them, by someone like them, and they all read it. Women and men, old and young, children, nuns, whores, soldiers, hospital patients, prisoners: everyone, really. An unbelievable phenomenon. It sold millions of copies in Italy and all around the world, and then there was a film."

As though stung by some unbearable thought, Monnanni suddenly snapped out of his contemplation of the sky and said that he had just been on the phone with the managing editor of the publishing house that had published *The Wolves Inside* way back in 1995, carefully specifying that those stentorian insults that I had overheard were not aimed at the managing editor but were meant for Vezzosi, who, by the way, was in need of a new assistant because the last one had left the job a few days ago.

And he asked me if I'd be interested.

"Me? But interested in doing what, Professor? Excuse me."

"In being his assistant."

"Assistant for what?"

"For writing."

"But didn't you say that he hasn't written anything for twenty-five years?"

"He writes, he writes. He doesn't publish, but he writes, that son of a bitch. Listen, you don't have any plans for lunch, do you? Because I'd like to take you to a nearby restaurant, to talk with my friend the publisher."

But he had already gotten up, already grabbed a worn-out suede jacket from the coatrack and opened the office door.

"Come on, let's go, he's probably there already."

The publisher was a short, chubby man who frugally introduced himself with just his surname, Passini.

"So, Emiliano, in theory the job is Monday through Friday, with Saturday and Sunday free, but the schedule is very flexible, that is, in substance, he decides, and at the last second. You'll stay at his house, a reconstructed farmhouse in the hills outside of Florence. You'll have a very comfortable room, with a bathroom and shower. Room and board are on him, you don't have to cook or clean your room, or even make your bed. Mamadou, his Central African personal assistant, takes care of all of that."

"A big oaf," Monnanni interjected, "that needs to be said."

Passini shot him a glance and then went on.

"You just have to help him write, the way he wants and when he wants, that's it. It could be that his requests might be, so to speak, rather unusual, but there is nothing to worry about. You can start right away, tomorrow even. I pay you, a thousand euros a month, net. In advance." And he pulled his checkbook out of his jacket.

The three of us were squeezed around a table for two in what might once have been a restaurant but was now a shabby lunch spot, and that day it was almost empty.

Surprised, I hesitated.

"Emiliano," whispered Monnanni, resting his hand on my forearm, "don't kick fortune in the teeth."

"Let's make it twelve hundred, okay?" offered Passini, who had put on a pair of funny-looking red glasses, filled out the check in minuscule handwriting, and handed it to me.

Up to that moment, the only check I'd ever seen was in a film, and that little slip of pastel-colored paper with my name written on it made a big impression on me. I immediately started imagining the scene of when I would show it to my mother and asking myself if it was better to surprise her, by leaving it on the kitchen table and waiting till she found it, or burst into the house running and brandish it like the spoils of war.

They were looking at me hopefully, the publisher and the professor, sitting on the edges of their imitation-cane beige plastic chairs as though those few seconds of shock were the sign of some uncertainty, as though the most hopeful person at that table wasn't me, who remembered that twelve hundred euros was double what any of the companies where I'd gone looking for work would have paid me, if they had hired me. No, more than double.

"I accept," I said, and then I folded the check in half and stuck it in the back pocket of my jeans.

"Very nice. And if it's all right with you I wouldn't bother writing up a contract or submitting invoices. Let's start like this and see how things go, okay?" Passini said, and he added that, as soon as I was able to find out, I was to report to him on the "state of the art" of the novel that Vezzosi was writing.

"What do you mean by 'state of the art'?"

"The title, the number of pages, and especially, though I realize this is difficult, a sort of percentage of how close it is to completion."

I smiled, incredulous.

"You mean you don't already know these things?"

The publisher looked, first at me and then at Monnanni, and said that, no, he didn't know those things, and that he couldn't ask Vezzosi about them because Vezzosi didn't want to tell him, and that, in essence, that was what he was paying me for. To find out. Fast.

"I'm sorry, but I don't understand."

"At this point, you'd better explain the whole thing to him," Monnanni said, and Passini sighed and, after making me promise that I would keep everything in the "most absolute and total confidence," he began telling me that the "small but prestigious Florentine publishing house" where he worked, and of which he was also one of the minority shareholders, had been waiting now for almost a quarter of a century for Vezzosi to deliver his second novel, whose very substantial advance had been paid in 1996 and then generously added to over the years, and whose imminent release had been announced four damn times and then postponed because each time the author had pulled back at the last moment.

"Offering the most grotesque and incredible excuses, Emiliano. I know them all by heart," Monnanni interjected. "The first time, he claimed that 'you can't impose the law of the chronometer on literature, a law valid only for the most reprehensible bourgeoisie.' The second, 'that it is totally impossible for me to deliver it, because the novel is not how I want it to be and maybe it never will be.' The third time, he said that 'by now I'm a man at the end of his rope and I don't believe in anything anymore, least of all in literature, and every novel seems to me only a desperate rifle shot into an empty sky.'"

"And the fourth time," Passini took over, "only a few weeks ago, he wrote to me that 'the novel is finally finished, but the last and fundamental sentence keeps slipping through my hands like spring water, and I categorically refuse to rush and risk ruining it only to bow to the impatient, obscene solicitations of some greedy fourth-rate typographer.'"

He shook his head as though he were shaking off a punch in the face, then he adjusted his glasses and continued:

"Up to this point, nothing strange, we've been waiting for over twenty years, we can wait another three months. Only that, out of the blue, a few weeks ago, my publishing house was bought by a very big publisher. A titan of the publishing industry. An arrogant, malevolent publishing giant, whose young managing editor comes to Florence and says that, if Vezzosi doesn't deliver his novel in time to be released in September, Christmas at the latest, our publishing house is toast, they'll close it and take the trademark to Milan, and I and the five dismayed women who work there will be fired on the spot."

"So, you understand, Emiliano," Monnanni added, "the importance of any information you can report."

And they fell silent. And looked at me.

"That is, excuse me, I'm supposed to play the spy."

"Oh no, Emiliano, come on," Monnanni blurted. "Spying has nothing to do with it."

"You just have to tell me if the novel exists," Passini said, "because at this point, I've got no certainty about anything. If it exists, as I hope, or rather as I'm sure it does, you have to find a way to read it and tell me if it's true that it's all there except for the last sentence. That's it. That doesn't seem to me like 'playing the spy.'"

Suddenly I saw myself rummaging through a desk, at night, in the silence of a strange house, in the dark, a flashlight in my mouth to keep my hands free. No, it was like stealing, and I wasn't a thief. It wasn't my thing. I took the check out of my pocket and, with death in my heart, held it out to him.

"I'm sorry, but I don't think I'm the right person for the job. I'm not a Judas."

Passini shook his head and looked at Monnanni.

"Now, you talk."

"Emiliano," the professor whispered, unsheathing a fervent tone that I had never heard him use, "there's something else that, at this point, I have to tell you. It's personal, very personal. I'm sorry to say that something very unfortunate has happened recently, extremely unfortunate. Life, with its dreadful force, has once again taken the upper hand in our miserable human affairs, and chance... blind, sneering chance... has decided to persecute..."

And Passini:

"Sauro, for God's sake, say it."

Monnanni looked me in the eye.

"Emiliano, the youngest of the dismayed women is pregnant."

"Ah... good for her. Best wishes."

"Best wishes, my ass, if you don't mind. She's pregnant by me," he mumbled, looking around that almost empty greasy spoon, then he hid his face in his hands and started moaning:

"What have I done, damn me, I'm fifty-six years old... How can I support her, the poor thing... And that innocent kid, poor soul, who'll raise it? If she loses her job all she'll have is me, and, let's face it, I've got nothing left to give... Nothing, not even love, no, especially love... And who knows if there even was love, if there ever was love... But what is love, if not a mirage, a cruel mirage... Oh, I can't go on like this, it's got to end soon. I'm at the end of the line, I've had it, I'm ready for the revolver. No, I've got nothing left, Emiliano, nothing. The little money I managed to put aside is all gone. All of it squandered,

thrown away on a thousand foolhardy choices . . . losing invest-
ments, goddam wining and dining. And who would have ever
thought that, against all odds, my sperm would still be so vig-
orous, so capable of fertilization? What kind of bestial instinct
are we governed by, tell me, what is it? Ah!"

With this final lament, Monnanni went silent. So he
wouldn't start up again, I turned to Passini:

"But why did they leave, the assistant that was there
before?"

"He was fired."

"For what?"

"Vezzosi found him rummaging through the papers on his
desk, at night, with a flashlight in his mouth. I never asked him
to do that, mind you, he did it all on his own. And so, he fired
him, and not in a very nice way."

"What do you mean?"

"Well, he was furious, and I can understand why. He's very
reserved, and he's jealous of his work."

"But what happened?"

"What happened is that he lost his head . . . and shot him."

"Shot him? Shot him how?"

Monnanni was staring at me, his hands clasped over his
mouth like the front legs of a praying mantis.

"But with salt, not with real bullets."

"It doesn't hurt all that bad, Emiliano, believe me."

"A little bit at first, but then it goes away."

Black Brother

. . .

I WOKE UP in Vezzosi's guest room when it was already past two in the afternoon, with a headache so vicious that I felt like taking an axe to my head like Zeus.

I staggered out of the room.

In the house, there wasn't a sound to be heard.

In the living room I found Mamadou reading, sitting on one of the twin armchairs bathed in sunlight in front of the window.

His short silver hair shining, spectacles sitting on the tip of his nose, he looked like one of those old ladies absorbed in her reading that Boccioni loved to paint before becoming a Futurist. I felt touched by that faded crimson T-shirt with ALABAMA written on it, khaki green military Bermudas, and the thongs dangling from his feet resting on the windowsill.

He looked defenseless, old, weak. A victim. Another Black man forced, by bigotry and the supreme injustice that has always governed the world, into serving always and in all ways a contemptuous and disturbed white man, who, as one of his little private jokes, forced him to wear a T-shirt with the name of America's most racist state.

"Good morning," I said, and he gave a start and jumped to his feet, book in hand. It was *Democracy* by Joan Didion. He hurriedly tore off his glasses, as if he were ashamed to have been seen wearing them, and he turned to me with a grimace.

"Fuck, you scared the hell out of me..."

I walked over to him and put a hand on his shoulder. He wasn't much taller than me.

"I'm sorry, Mamadou, Black brother...for last night, too. I don't know what happened. I lost control, and now I regret having said all those things, the ones I said about you, too. I thought them, sure, and I still think them, but I certainly should have figured out another way to say them. I really behaved like a lout, and I'd like to apologize to Vezzosi as well. You know, the fact is I'm not used to drinking alcohol, and these past few days have been really rough, actually, these past few months, and, well, I'm really sorry. Could you please tell me where Mr. Vezzosi is? I'd like to apologize in person and say good-bye, and then quickly go away because it doesn't seem like—"

I didn't even see it. I felt the impact and heard the sharp sound of the slap coming from my left cheek. My head jolted to the side; I lost my balance and found myself sitting on the floor, looking up at Mamadou towering above me, his earring sparkling. He didn't look like one of Boccioni's old ladies anymore.

"You are now officially excused, white brother..."

I looked at him and tried to get up, but I couldn't do it. My head was spinning, I felt feeble. He helped me pull myself up and escorted me to the bathroom. It was a struggle to walk, my legs were trembling, my cheek was burning.

"Come on, let's go, I hardly even touched you. Throw some water on your face..."

He closed the door and left me there, leaning on the sink. I looked in the mirror. I was unrecognizable, behold the man: hair disheveled, shirt buttoned wrong, my left cheek red from the wallop I'd just received. But why, why? What had happened? What had I done? And where had I ended up? What was I doing there, anyway? What a disaster! And what a fucked-up life, damn it!

I shut my eyes, and I kept them shut until it felt like my head was getting back together; then I washed my face, smoothed my hair back into some sort of order, rebuttoned my shirt, and opened the door. Mamadou was outside waiting for me. He gave me an icy stare, his arms folded across his chest.

"Now, tell me what made you think you could insult someone like Vezzosi, you, who aren't good enough to even lick his shoes...Look, he's not at all like what you think he is, he's had a really hard life...You don't know him, don't know anything about him, you're just a fuckin' smart-ass little twerp! You've got no respect; you think you know everything and you don't know nothin' about nothin'...And all of that hate, where the hell does that come from, huh? What did they do to you that you're so damn angry? Because however badly they've treated you, they've treated me thirty times worse, but you don't hear me cryin' and complainin', and sayin' everything sucks, you understand? Hey, you get that, or not?"

He was fired up, and I was afraid another wallop was on the way. I lowered my eyes.

"Look. If it was up to me, I'd kick your ass out of here in a minute, but for some reason, he likes you, the Maestro, and he wants you to stay. But for now, get your ass out of here, move it, and don't come back till I call you!"

I raised my eyes and looked at him, surprised.

"Stay? What do you mean, stay? I'm not staying even if…"

He wasn't expecting that.

"What?"

Seeing him speechless, maybe even disappointed, encouraged me, and so I upped the ante, because it's one thing not to be proud, and it's another thing to suffocate it forever, and I had always suffocated my pride, but in that moment, I couldn't take it anymore.

"I'm leaving, and right now. I mean, as fast as I can…"

"What are you saying? You can't leave."

"Sure, I can, I'm not a prisoner here. Where's Vezzosi?"

"He's gone. Left for London."

"For London? When? This morning?"

"Yes, this morning."

"Well then, you say good-bye for me."

I left him there and went back to my room to get my stuff together, put the book of Epictetus in my backpack, and strutted out of the house, walking right past him.

"Wait a minute, Emiliano, come on…"

I didn't stop, didn't answer him, and didn't even say good-bye.

I got on my scooter and left. A hidden electric eye blinked and the gate swung open silently, and I shot down the mule path happy as I'd been only a few times in my life, while the wind caressed my face and hair because in my rush to get away, I'd forgotten to put my helmet on.

I was free! I was victorious, and what a victory it was!

I'd told him where to get off, the *Maestro*. I'd let it all hang out. I'd made him the target for all of my righteous anger and he had been so struck by what I'd said that he wasn't even able to respond! I'd shut him up, goddamn it!

Because I was not some trembling servant like all the others and I didn't need him at all, and I had no fear for the future because suddenly I could see it there before me, clear as day. As soon as I got back to Florence I would go straight to the university and enroll in the master's program in Philology, Literature, and History that I had stupidly given up on, and I would graduate with highest honors, and if, to pay my way, I had to unload cases of fruit at the wholesale market, I would unload cases of fruit at the wholesale market, and then I would win a competition for a teaching position in a classical high school, and any classical high school would be fine for

me, wherever, even one in the country, if there are still classical high schools in the country, and I would get engaged to
Allegra, and we would get married, and together with her I
would dedicate my life to explaining the Ancients to girls and
boys, and maybe we would have one of our own, a boy or a girl.
That's how it was going to go, and as for Vezzosi, and all of his
bullshit, I wouldn't give a fuck!

With Mamadou, things hadn't gone quite as well, but he
was a tough nut to crack, and anyway, he was not happy that
I'd left. He had been sure I would stay on to obey him like
a dog, and instead: *So long, Mamadou! Until we never meet
again!*

I laughed, imagining Vezzosi's disappointment on find-
ing out he would no longer have an assistant and, who knows,
maybe even getting angry with Mamadou. He would send
him to my house to beg me to come back, and I would greet
him in the living room, surrounded by smiling pictures of
my father, I'd offer him a cup of coffee and then I would say
to him, very gently: *No, thank you, Mamadou, really,* and as
he closed the door behind him, I would add something like,
*But, you know,…if you hadn't given me that slap, maybe, just
maybe, I could have changed my mind, but by now it's water over
the dam. Bye-bye, and please give my best to your "Maestro,"* and
then he would start down the stairs with his head bowed, defeated…But who cared, anyway, about Mamadou! He was
just another of those imbeciles who had been slapping me
around ever since middle school. Let's just erase him from

memory and send him to oblivion, Emiliano, come on! *Ad maiora!* On to greater things!

As I was brushing those curves like Valentino Rossi, I decided that as soon as I got home, I would call Allegra to tell her everything—oh God, almost everything—and I would ask her out for coffee, and this time she would come, I was sure of it, because from now on everything was going to go my way, and then some…

And then I remembered the book for my mother.

I slammed on the brakes. The scooter skidded to the side and I came close to sliding off the road and down the embankment.

Fuck, I forgot it back there.

I banged my fist against the handlebar, hurting myself in the process. As much as I hated the idea of going back to that house just minutes after leaving it in victory, I couldn't go back home to Mama without her copy, and the longer I waited the more hassle it would be. So, I turned the bike around and I started back down the mule path very, very slowly. In front of the gate, I called him on the phone.

"Sorry, Mamadou, it's Emiliano…I forgot something. Can you open the gate?"

No answer, but the gate opened wide in silence and I walked slowly back up the lawn, the enthusiasm of my escape now faded. I couldn't even remember where it was. I'd had it in my hand when we were on the terrace, but then I'd lost all trace of it.

Mamadou was waiting for me at the door, with the usual folded arms. I put the bike up on the kickstand, walked past him without looking at him, and went inside. I looked on the veranda, in the living room, in the dining room, every place I'd been, but it wasn't there.

"I don't suppose you've seen my mother's book?"

"Did you look in your room, Emiliano? You know, where I carried you on my back last night?"

It wasn't possible, but I went up the stairs anyway, and there it was, on the bedside table. How could I not have seen it, shit . . . I tried too quickly to grab it and it fell out of my hand. The corner of the hard cover hit the floor and the book opened up. I picked it up and, as I was leafing through it to make sure the spine had not come unglued, I noticed at the bottom of the title page a curlicued signature. Right above it was written:

> *To my dear Franca,*
> *mother of my friend*
> *Zapata*

I sat down on the bed to read it, and reread it. I'd told Vezzosi where to get off, sure. I'd let it all hang out. I'd made him the target for all of my righteous anger, and his reprisal had been to do me a favor. The emperor of the bullies, the shithead that shot salt at his assistants, had taken it upon himself to make sure I didn't make a bad showing with my mother.

Now I didn't know what to do, because I'm somebody who is content with very little and every gift always seems too much to me, but given the circumstances this really was too much. Lots of stuff, as Allegra used to say.

My friend Zapata.

I could still up and leave, and surely that would have been fair, but how could I then go on telling myself I was the innocent one, who escapes heroically from his unjust imprisonment, the oppressed youth, who rebels against the powerful and shakes off his chains? If I left, I would be the chicken stealer who makes a quick getaway with the stolen goods in his dirty, sweaty hands.

Yet, how could I stay after everything that had happened?

I stayed there in the room for a long while, not knowing what to do, sitting on the bed looking at the arabesques in the carpet, and then I heard Mamadou rummaging around in the kitchen, and all of a sudden my heart went out to them, to him and Vezzosi, voluntary recluses in that isolated blockhouse, solitary as dogs, without anything to do from morning to night, with no friends and no women they didn't have to pay afterwards, sought after only by people who wanted something from them, accustomed to eating and drinking delicacies, whose goodness they couldn't share with anyone, condemned to living each day in an empty, sterile land of Bengodi with which they must certainly be bored to tears, for as long as they had been living there, and all this only because they were incapable of facing the outside world, which they no doubt must be afraid of, maybe even more so than me. With all of their power and all of their arrogance, they had shut themselves up in a cocoon, and right then and there I was sorry that life had treated them so badly, so such so that I almost had tears in my eyes.

I know, I'm crazy. But that's the way I am.

I went down the stairs and into the kitchen, the book in hand, and found Mamadou slowly pouring coffee from an old espresso pot into one of those greasy white cups from a coffee bar.

"He signed the book for my mother..."

He took a swig of mineral water to prepare his mouth as the Neapolitans do, and he started sipping his coffee. Then he nodded, without deigning to look at me.

"I saw that. It's been twenty years since he last signed a book for someone. What the fuck he sees in you, I really don't think I'll ever understand..."

He was one pugnacious asshole, Mamadou. If he weren't Black, I would have said Fascist. But there aren't any Black Fascists, right? Or maybe, yes? Well, I've never figured that out... He had given me a wallop that *had turned my head around*, as my father used to say, he had laughed at me and permitted himself to call me an ignorant jerk, he, who was one of the self-taught, who was a caregiver for a nut and had always lived a life of bullying. We would never have gotten along. He didn't like me and I didn't like him.

"So, what have you decided?"

'I'll stay," I heard myself say. And what did that son of a bitch do then? He shot me that irresistible smile of his, and *sighed*.

"As Goethe said, and was later cited by the master Lowry in the epigraph to his *Volcano*...*Whosoever unceasingly strives upward...him we can save*...Now, go back home, get. I'll call you when the Maestro returns from London."

And he went into the living room, coffee cup in hand, to read.

Backs Against the Wall

· · ·

WHEN I DELIVERED the book to my mother, she read the dedication and held it to her heart, then she excused herself and, her eyes welling up with tears, took refuge in her bedroom and didn't come back out until the next morning, while I was calling the university to enroll in the master's program and a recorded voice was telling me that they would not be accepting applications until September.

There followed two empty days, during which I did little else other than settle back into my immobile life and start getting anxious about the months of an overly long summer, whose present to me would be a few remedial lessons for the freckle-faces and fading hopes for winning back Allegra. Total boredom, in other words, and the anxiety of delusion in the offing, titanic and inevitable.

Then, on the morning of the third day, while I was watching the videos of the immense waves crashing against the sides of a tanker on the high seas, Monnanni rang my doorbell. I went downstairs and found him standing in front of the con-dominium gate, his fingers clutching the bars, by his side a young, very pregnant woman in a flowery dress with a dis-gruntled look on her face.

"Emiliano, thank God you're here. I clambered up that obscene goat path twice at the risk of being shot at by that damn killer, but forget about it... I'm sorry for showing up here like this, but it's of the utmost importance that I speak to you right away, face-to-face, because time is getting short, and by now we've got our backs against the wall: we've got to know about the novel and you're our only resource and last hope..."

And he got down on his knees, pulling down by her arm the young, very pregnant woman with the flowery dress and the disgruntled look on her face so that she would get down on her knees too, ignoring her feeble protests.

"But no, Professor, what are you doing..."

His knees down on the filthy sidewalk, his hands joined together, his eyes fixed on mine, Monnanni whispered feverishly:

"Son, your old professor is begging you... Go back up there and carry out the enterprise this very night, under cover of darkness, impelled by the courage and bravado of youth and by the ardor and immortal example of the heroes Eury-alus and Nisus... Do it, I implore you, do it, or all will be for naught, and the maelstrom of poverty and desperation will swallow us all, the guilty and the innocent..."

I was about to respond that Euryalus and Nisus had died, however, while they were carrying out their enterprise, when Monnanni became petrified and started staring at something behind my back. I turned around, and my mother was there, looking at us.

The professor went silent and struggled back up on his feet, helped by the young, very pregnant woman, then he greeted my mother with a reedy voice, said he had to go, took the girl under his arm, and they got back into their gray economy car with the dent in the side.

"I beg you, Emiliano," said the young, very pregnant woman, leaning her head out the window as they slowly drove off, with horrendous screeches of metal against metal, "please do something…"

My mother held out the bag of trash to me.

"Please take this to the dumpster, Emiliano… But what happened to your professor? Who is that girl? His daughter? Come on, hurry up, everything's ready."

When we were sitting at the dinner table, she felt she had to apologize.

"I'm very sorry about that little breakdown I had the other night, Emiliano, but I want to explain to you that I had it for a reason… You have to know that *The Wolves Inside* was a book your father liked, too, and some nights, when we were newlyweds, before you were born, we would sit in the living room and turn off the TV, and he would read to me aloud from it…"

She paused, teary-eyed, and gestured to me not to say anything.

"I'm sorry, I'm sorry...I just wanted to tell you that this affectionate dedication, even if it seems like nothing to you, would have made him so happy, that's all, and not just me...because I haven't lost my mind, and I'm not acting like a young girl, that's what I mean..."

Of course not, Mama...I'm the one who should apologize..."

And then she asked me if I was okay, because I was *so gloomy*.

I said, yes, sure I was okay, but it wasn't true.

There was a worm eating at me.

Actually, two.

The first worm was that I had woken up convinced I had acted badly with Vezzosi, and that I needed to apologize to him immediately, because with my father we had decided many years ago that if someone acted badly toward us, and there was no doubt that Vezzosi had behaved badly toward me, we were nevertheless not authorized to respond in kind. Ever. No matter what. No reprisals, no vendettas, because reprisals and vendettas are the stuff of imbeciles and spoilsports.

He and I would always behave well, no matter what might happen. And if we ever acted badly, we had to apologize right away. We joked about having our code of behavior, and we had fun debating about whether this or that thing was acceptable for our code. It had nothing to do with morality or religion—Dad didn't go to Mass. We did it for ourselves. So we could be at peace with ourselves, in every moment of our lives. In this world of assholes, he and I would be the good guys.

But, that night, I had behaved badly.

First of all, I had taken the book of Epictetus, and that was inexcusable and shameful because there is no breed worse than book stealers. Plus, where did I get off going to someone's house as a guest and then starting to insult the people who had invited me? There was also a job involved, and I had said he was the symbol of everything that was wrong with the world, that he was like Mr. Magoo...But why? What was the need for that? And all that vehemence, that arrogance, where did they come from? What was I thinking, that I was *enlightening him? Doing justice?*

He had let me go on with that whole tirade without interrupting me, without responding even once, and with a smile on his face...Why hadn't he defended himself? Certainly, he must have thought I was an imbecile with whom it wasn't even worth trying to reason...A smart-ass little twerp, as Mamadou had said...But then, why had he told me that I was perfect? Perfect for what? And why had he wanted me to stay? And why, then, had he written that affectionate dedication to my mother?

The second worm was what had happened in that disco. I tried not to think about it, but I *had gone whoring.* Not of my own free will, certainly. They had taken me there. But nobody had grabbed me by the neck and forced me to rub up against that little girl of undetermined nationality who must have been my age, if not younger; a poor soul, exploited and oppressed, the guiltless daughter of a moral and material misery that I couldn't even imagine, a sensitive and kind person who had trusted me to the point of falling asleep on top of me—a victim, whom I had had no scruples about victimizing, too, just the opposite, in fact, I couldn't wait to get my hands on her and I had spilled my semen in that whorehouse where I had also engaged in illicit transactions, albeit by way of a third party, because Vezzosi had surely paid for the service—let's put it this way—that I was rendered, and therefore, I had to confess, and right away, but how could I recount all this to Father Santino? Could I put the blame on the gin and tonics and the wine?

Mama asked me if I had a fever.

"Your eyes are glassy, Emiliano."

I denied it, told her I felt like a king, and then the phone rang. It was Passini, all bent out of shape. He was shouting.

"Why the fuck didn't you tell me that Vezzosi is going to Milan on Sunday to speak at a clothing fair?"

"What?"

"Tell me why, damn it!"

"No, he's in London, visiting his daughter…"

"Don't give me that bullshit! That's not possible! Vezzosi is a nutcase who hasn't gone out of the house for twenty years, even the birds know that, and you're trying to double-cross me, and that's not right because I'm paying you, you got that? Now, tell me, is it true or not? Is he going to Milan, or not? Because on the fucking internet everybody and his brother is talking about it."

"Honestly, I don't know anything about this thing in Milan, Professor, I swear it, plus the internet is full of fantasy stories and fake news, don't worry about it. What they're writing is not true... But if you don't trust me, ask Mamadou, or call the fair, I'm sorry, somebody there must know about it, whether it's true or not..."

"Mamadou hasn't responded to me for ten years, and I've already called the fair... which is actually the Milan Fair, and they told me that it's all organized, and they've already sold *two thousand* tickets."

"Well then," I said, my mouth dry, "that's how things stand."

And Passini, his voice trembling with desperation:

"But no, you don't understand. If it's true, it's a disaster, a tragedy... Vittorio will never, I mean never, go on a trip to Milan to speak to two thousand people, that's just not possible, there are no two ways about it... And, if by some divine miracle, he should really make it onto that stage, what would he talk about? He doesn't know anything. He's ignorant, just like all writers are... He's still stuck back in the 1990s, he has no idea how the world has changed, and he has no idea how to speak in public, because he's never done it... No, he won't go, you'll see, and he's going to disappoint all those people who've bought tickets to hear him, and I don't want to know who they are, because no one in Italy buys books anymore, shit...And they'll be furious with him, and he won't be everyone's pet writer anymore, but just a shithead who dumps on his readers, and they'll start to hate him, and then, yes, then it really will be all over. Who is it that started spreading the word about this damn event in Milan, anyway? Who? You or that African psychopath? Who, tell me! Because it couldn't have been anyone else but you two, fuck, go fuck yourselves..."

And he hung up.

Ten minutes later, he called again, all meek and mild. Another person.

"Emiliano, listen to me, so it's all confirmed. Vittorio is really going to Milan. I don't know how it's possible, but I heard it from Zucchi, and if she says it, that's how it is."

"Who is she, this Zucchi?"

"Drop it. At this point, it's absolutely essential that you go to Milan, too. Understand?"

"Me?"

"Yes, of course, you absolutely have to, and during the trip you've got to film the whole thing with your cell and send everything by email to this person I'm about to have you talk to. He's a big expert in digital communications and he'll take care of sharing the images on social media...We're going do a big promo for the new novel, and for the old one, too, while we're at it..."

"But, excuse me, Passini...Have you spoken to Vezzosi about this? And does Mamadou know about the filming? Because I doubt he'd be real excited about it...You don't really think I could film it on the sly, do you?"

"But you've got to do it, Emiliano, any way you can."

"It's not possible, Passini, believe me."

"Emiliano, no offense, but I really have to tell you this. You're not someone who solves problems, there...Just the opposite, you're someone who creates them. I'm sorry to have to say this, but that's how it is. You always make trouble, shit doubts on everything. You can't get anywhere that way, don't you know that?"

Incredibly enough, I was offended.

"That could be, Professor Passini. So, look, let's do this...Why don't you come along and film Vezzosi under Mamadou's nose, okay? But have yourself followed by an ambulance with a medic on board, because that guy is going to beat your brains out, you got that?"

There was a long pause.

"Emiliano, please. I'm asking you for a favor, help me. I'm begging you...I'll have the expert call you right away. He knows what to do, he's been in a lot of situations like this. Ask him, be nice. His name is Gabriel, like the Archangel. Thanks. Ciao."

And he hung up again. Ten minutes later, the phone rang again.

"Emiliano, ciao, this is Gabriel. You've got to tell him that the photos are a gift to the world, and the videos precious testimony of his contribution to contemporary Italian culture, even European and worldwide culture. You have to fawn over him, tell him he's the greatest. That works every time, with everybody. But take the pictures with the phone horizontal, make sure, and the videos, too, otherwise you can't see a damn thing, understand?"

"Good morning, Gabriel, but I'm not the problem and neither is Vezzosi. There's this character that acts as his man Friday who doesn't want us to take pictures…"

"Who is it? A bodyguard?"

"I don't know. I suppose you could call him that, yes…"

"Fine, so give him some money. Bodyguards are real ball-breakers, but then they always take the money."

"No, look, you don't know this guy. Plus, I don't have any money…"

"Oh, well… But why is he famous, this Vezzosi?"

"He's a writer."

"And since when are writers famous? They're throwbacks to the Stone Age, writers, from the Jurassic!"

"He's pretty famous among people my parents' age. A long time ago he wrote a book that was a bestseller."

"Yeah, yeah, let me see… I'm looking… Oh… *The Wolves Inside,* he wrote that? We had a copy in the house, I remember. I even seem to recall reading some pieces of it, as a kid, while I was taking a shit. So, he was really famous after all, our Vezzosi… but back in the days of Anchises…"

"Anchises was great."

"Banged Aphrodite."

"Exactly."

"So you did the classical, too, Emiliano?"

"Why, are there other schools?"

"Ah, but look, there's some coke involved here, too... Not that we need it, it gives it a negative spin, but it adds weight. But why has he become a hermit? He's got a new book coming out, right? We could turn it into something like the Return of the Monster from the Black Lagoon... The wicked and ingenious junkie that comes back clean and repentant... Or no, unrepentant..."

"I wouldn't focus too much on the novel..."

"Why not?"

"We're not so sure that it's done."

"Ah, right, fantastic... He's not even on the social networks, this Vezzosi. Not one. Oh, why do they always give me the easy jobs?"

"There's an old interview, on YouTube..."

"We can't use it, it's flat, there's only that stuff about the cocaine. We don't have anything, damn it! Got to invent something, and we need something fresh, news-cyclable... But, you know, to look at, he's not bad, I mean, he wasn't bad, at thirty. Now, how is he?"

"No, now he's old, puffy-faced and flabby. A real butterball."

"Humpty Dumpty?"

"No, but anyway he's no handsome prince. Not in the least. But I have to say that, for some unknown reason, he appeals to women. There are some videos of his women read-ers that..."

"Ah, yeah, I see...Women who are moved to tears...We can start from there, then. Where is he going to speak? At the 1980s Fair, good, we can use that...Nostalgia is perfect, really strong. Come on, let's go, take a picture of him and let's see how it looks. That's how we'll start..."

"I can't. He's in London, and I don't have any pictures of him."

"What, you don't have any pictures of him? Come on, that can't be: you work for him, he's famous, and you've never taken his picture? Where is it that you are? Instagram for sure. Name?"

"Emiliano De Vito."

"What kind of name is that? Sounds like something out of a film with Totò. Don't you have a nickname?"

"Vezzosi calls me Zapata."

"Better than nothing. We'll use that instead of Emiliano De Vito. But look, you're a crazy poster...What's this, all pic-tures of sunsets?"

"They're not sunsets, they're sunrises."

"All the same...What a bore, no wonder you've got forty followers...But these pix aren't so bad after all, you know? You're not bad. You've got taste. Pretty melancholy, this fuck-ing profile, though, cries like cut vines...Shit, oh, there's also a cemetery...Come on, get with it, send me a picture of this Vezzosi, you've got to have one..."

"Listen, Gabriel, I've got a photo, but I can't send it to you."

"What the fuck, I ask you for a picture, that who knows what it's like and that surely I won't be able to use, and you won't give it to me? No way...Hey, I'm the Archangel, people come looking for me and they ask me on their knees to help them...big names, that I'm not at liberty to tell you right now, but believe me, very, very big names. Come on, do the right thing, send me the picture."

"I promised I wouldn't show it to anyone."

"Christ, I don't believe it, I feel like I'm back in middle school..."

"Well, that's the way I am..."

"I got it. And actually I like you. You're one hell of a wimp, but you know about Anchises, and I respect you. You know that I've been giving people that line for years and no one has ever gotten it? You're the first, shit, and so I can't tell you to go fuck yourself, on the contrary, I want to give you a hand to polish up this deeply sad profile, but now you've got to send me the picture..."

And that's when I thought: *Why not?* What's the big deal about one picture?...And really, if he didn't want his picture taken, he wouldn't have let them snap it...

"Okay, I'll send it to you, but you've got to crop me out. Because I'm in it, too."

"What is it, a fucking selfie?"

"Yeah, promise me you'll cut me out."

"Sure, I'll cut you. What can I do with you?"

I sent it to him.

"I got it. Okay. It's not bad. Maybe we can use it...Hey, he's good-looking, this Vezzosi...a real old gent, *old school*, a classic alpha male, whiskey and left hooks...This guy crunches, take it from the Archangel. You, brother, on the other hand, I'm sorry to tell you, crunch a lot less. But let's do the whole thing from your profile, that way you'll be someone, too. Maybe. Gimme the password."

"Of my profile?"

"Sure. You're going to be with him, aren't you? Aren't you coming to Milan together? Let's do an *on the road* number, like Che and his buddy on the Poderosa. Come on, gimme the password."

"Archangel, I'll give it to you, but I mean it..."

"What do you care, you can always go back to your sunsets and your cemeteries anytime you want, no? You need to generate some activity...You've got forty followers, and with forty followers you don't get laid. If I can get you up to five thousand followers, maybe you can get laid, too...Maybe even with this Allegra97..."

I swallowed.

"How do you know about Allegra?"

"Easy, you put a like on everything she posts, even this picture of the wet dog...Gimme the password, come on..."

"Okay, the password is...but it's the one I put in when I was a kid, when I started, and I've never changed it, so don't laugh..."

"I promise."

"MythicalEmi. But with a capital E."

"Hahahahahahahahahhahahah! Fantastic!"

"You promised…"

"But no, come on, I'm laughing because I had a password with 'mythical' in it, too, when I started! 'Mythicalgabriel' was mine! Awesome, Emi!"

"But how old are you, Gabriel?"

"Twenty-two. And you?"

"Me, too! So, we can do away with all the formalities, then."

"Sure, but it really made me laugh when you talked to me like I was some kind of higher-up … Oh, bro, for that thing I said to you before, don't let it get you down. I'm not a cruncher either, you know? I'm like you. And I used to have forty followers, too, but then I started getting it together … I'm sure not Anchises, but I'd be happy to have you take a look at some of the ones I've done … Yeah, why not, tomorrow I'll send you a picture or two … Ciaoooo …"

Allegra

. . .

"WHY DIDN'T YOU tell me that Vezzosi is speaking Sunday morning in Milan?"

She hadn't even sat down yet. She was standing there in front of me looking grumpy, her gray eyes flashing lightning bolts, and me thinking that I really loved her as I had never loved her before, and it mattered nothing to me if they said she wasn't pretty, to me she was beautiful; and it mattered nothing to me if she wasn't tall and thin and blonde, because she was the only woman for me, as that song said.

"Ciao, Allegra, I'm really, really glad to see you."

"Me too," she said, and sat down. Then she asked me who was going to pay, because she had five euros in her pocket, and when I announced that there was no problem because I was now a working man, she relaxed and started tapping on her phone screen.

A waiter came over, a non-Italian guy around our age. She ordered a coffee and I ordered a tonic with ice.

"With a wedge of one of those special green lemons, please," I added, after a frenetic internal debate with myself over whether I should say it or not.

"You mean a lime?"

"Yeah, right, I think so…"

"Comin' right up," he said, and went off.

Lime, that's it, of course. What a dumbass! Special green lemon…I can't believe it…Allegra was sneering.

"So, Emiliano? You don't have anything to tell me about Vezzosi? It's all over the place, this thing…"

"What are you talking about?"

She started reading from her phone.

"After twenty-five years of total silence, Vittorio Vezzosi, the hermit of Italian literature and its undisputed and undisputable alpha male, will be speaking Sunday in Milan at the official opening of *SuperVintage19! The Market-Fair of the Eighties and Nineties*, before an audience of unfathomable dimensions…"

She looked at me for a second, and then continued reading.

"When the news broke, the phones at the fair were immediately overwhelmed by his fans and especially by his female fans, and demand for tickets was so high that the seats in the hall that had been chosen to host the event were sold out in half an hour, forcing the organization to opt for a larger hall, but in no time, that one was sold out as well, and so, having received some five thousand requests, it was decided to hold the much awaited *lectio magistralis*—whose enigmatic but undoubtedly intriguing title is 'Anchises in the 1980s'—in the arena of the Milan Fair, the enormous space that hosts rock concerts and motocross races..."

She took her eyes off the screen, and stared at me point-blank.

"So?"

"But I don't know anything about it, Allegra, believe me, really...I mean, I know that it actually might happen, this thing, but they still haven't given me any confirmation."

"So, what kind of secretary are you, then?"

"I am not his secretary."

"I was kidding, come on, I know that...But I would really like to come, to hear him in Milan..."

"No kidding? Since when do you care so much about Vezzosi?"

"Get a load of this!...Since I feel like it, okay? No, really, I'll tell you the truth, after your message the other day, I started rereading the book, and I liked it a lot better than the first time, and I talked with my girlfriends about it and found out that they all had read it, too...And now we're all in love with him..."

"In love with him?"

"Oh yes! He's a really good-looking man...Don't look at me like that, Emiliano...Someone might say you were jealous..."

The waiter arrived with the coffee and the tonic.

"Jealous?" I whispered when he left. "Me? Oh, come on. And, sorry, but you guys maybe don't realize that you're looking at pictures from thirty years ago... Today, he's different, totally different..."

"Oh yeah? Now, tell me he's not a cool dude..."

She showed me her phone, and on the home page of Milan's newspaper, the *Corriere*, there was the picture of Vezzosi that I had sent the Archangel. He had cropped me out of it. Amazingly, incredibly, right then I was sorry not to be in it, too.

"Sorry, Allegra, but what do you mean, *cool dude*? He's an old man, and fat, with white hair...What's cool about him?"

"First of all, his hair's not white, if anything, gray, and anyway he's sexy as hell, Vezzosi... You really don't understand anything about women, I mean, you know, nothing whatsoever. He's a legend, your boss."

"I don't have a boss."

"Okay, are you taking me to Milan, or not?"

"Allegra, listen... Vezzosi hasn't said anything to me about a gig in Milan. And besides, he's in London..."

"In London? What's he doing in London?"

"His daughter is in school there."

"He must be a wonderful father... You've got it so nice, being so close to him. What's he like in person?"

I shrugged. It wasn't supposed to go like this.

"Huh, let's just say that knowing him is not all that cool."

"Oh, yeah, that must be really true... Thousands of people all over Italy are going to Milan to hear him speak, and he's no big deal... I don't think you get it, Emiliano, just who you're working for."

"Believe me, I get it. Totally."

"No, I don't think so. You haven't even read the book."

"So what?"

"So everything. It's all there."

"What do you mean?"

"If you read it, you get it... A writer talks with his books... You're too proud, Emiliano... You could learn so much from him, I mean tons, really. You are so lucky, remember that. You're privileged."

"Me, privileged?"

"Yeah, you. Like all males. Why didn't he pick me to be his assistant instead of you, huh? Because the world belongs to men..."

I faked a big laugh.

"You don't know what you're talking about. Really..."

"No, I know perfectly. It's you that doesn't get it..."

I blew some air out of my mouth and there was a long pause. We always end up fighting, she and I. Every damn time, shit! She drank down her coffee in two quick gulps.

"So, are you taking me to Milan, or not?"

"If I go, too, yeah. If not, I'll find you a ticket, and you can go alone. Don't worry."

"I've got three friends."

"Okay. I'll find tickets for them, too."

She lowered her eyes for a second, then looked at me.

"Why don't you come too?"

"Ahhh, I don't know... It's all fucked up, Allegra, I... But, sure, if you're going then I should figure out a way to come too, no?"

"Yeah, and maybe you can introduce me to him."

"Sure, we're friends..."

"Okay, thanks... You're sweet."

She gave me a caress, and I didn't like it at all. I smiled bitterly.

"I meant that we're friends, me and Vezzosi, but maybe you thought I was saying we were friends, you and I... And I guess that's true, too. We're all friends, Allegra. Bosom buddies."

"Idiot," she said, shaking her head, and went back to digiting on her phone.

He Wants to Go to Milan

● ● ●

JUST BEFORE DINNER, Mamadou called me.

"The Maestro says you've got to be at the house tomorrow morning at nine. Make sure you're on time, because he wants to leave early for Milan, and I won't be there...I'm sure it'll turn out that he doesn't go anywhere, but if he does actually go, you've got to go with him because he is absolutely incapable of traveling alone, got it?"

"No, sorry, didn't he just go to London?"

"No."

"What do you mean, no?"

"No. He didn't go."

"But you told me..."

"Okay, Emiliano, this is something that is just between us: the Maestro is not well, understand? He's got some problems, and not just now, but ever since they started breaking his balls about finishing the novel it's been getting worse..."

"Problems? What problems?"

"Several problems. And then he gets panic attacks."

"Really?"

"Yes. He shuts down and starts to shake. That's the sign. He shakes. No, first he stutters and then he shakes. Sometimes he faints, too, but it's nothing, I mean, it's not serious. You give him fifteen drops of Xanax and he goes right back to normal, but then he feels terrible about having had the attack, and he's ashamed of himself and locks himself in his room and doesn't come out for days...Don't ever talk to him about it, about the panic attacks, not for any reason, otherwise they come back, got it?"

"Yeah, I got it. But what am I supposed to do?"

"If he wants to go to Milan, you have to go with him."

"But how can he go to Milan? Hasn't it been twenty years that he hasn't been out of the house?"

"No, that's Passini's bullshit. He gives everybody that story, the jerk...You've seen yourself that he goes out, no? He doesn't go out often and when he does he always goes to the same places, but he goes out, sure he goes out. Even on his own, sometimes. Around here, he goes out to buy fish, or prosciutto...In the summer he even takes a ride on the motorcycle...Without a helmet, naturally, because he says it's an affront to his personal freedom, and by now the carabinieri don't even pull him over anymore..."

My mother appeared before me, leaning against the doorjamb, and stayed there, staring at me. She was smiling.

"Before, he used to go to the movies, to the early show, but then he stopped. Every once in a while, he asks me to take him to the sea, to his friend Genova. He goes for a swim, and then they sit on the beach for hours, talking about books and fish. But he hasn't been to Florence alone for twenty years or so, since that time he got sick at the 'Costume Football' match…"

I made a questioning gesture to Mama, who was still looking at me and smiling, and I had to take my eyes off her not to lose track of the phone conversation, which I then realized I had already lost.

"And so … sorry, Mamadou … you were saying that he didn't go to London…"

"No."

"And what did he do these past few days?"

"Nothing, he stayed in his room the whole time."

"Oh, sure. After that night out…"

"Oh, listen here, where do you get off talking about that night out? Shit, I've never seen anyone get that drunk, Mary, Mother of God, you even made trouble there in the disco…"

I swallowed.

"Really? What did I do?"

"Ask the Maestro what you did and what you said… Anyway, we dropped you at home and we went directly to the airport to catch the first plane, the seven a.m., because he thought it would be easier to leave when he was sleepy, you know… Sleep the whole flight and wake up in London… He bought a ticket, and up to that point everything was fine, but then he panicked at check-in, like always…"

"Is he afraid of flying?"

"No, it's not that... It bothers him when they ask him for his passport..."

"What?"

"Yeah, because Vittorio has an authority problem... I mean, he can't stand being in a situation where someone tells him what he has to do, you know? When he doesn't feel free..."

"So, what happened?"

"What always happens. He started stuttering and saying he wanted to go back home, and I tried to calm him down, but he got more agitated and then the police came, and they wanted to arrest me because they thought I was the one causing trouble, and he got pissed off and called them racists... It was pretty much of a mess and we came close to being arrested, the both of us... And in the end, he didn't leave again this time."

"..."

"..."

"So, then, tomorrow morning what should I do?"

"Get there early, before nine, and see how he is, and then I don't know, Emiliano... You'll deal with it, what can I say?"

"Sorry, but you're not going to be there?"

"No, I told you. I'm leaving. Going back to Africa, otherwise, they'll deport me."

"How's that?"

"It's because of the complaint filed by your colleague... wounds and threats, can you believe it? He's such an idiot, I'm telling you..."

"But you shot at him..."

"Yeah, but with salt, come on, and in the ass, not at his face, even though in his case they coincide…"

"But what do you mean, they'll deport you?"

"If someone gets accused of wounding someone, the carabinieri have to investigate, and, in fact, they called me to come into the barracks tomorrow, but I can't go because I'm undocumented, I don't have permission to stay, and so I'm not going…But if I don't go, they'll come to get me, and if they catch me without permission to stay, I become an illegal and they arrest me and take me to one of those holding camps, and then they kick my ass out of Italy, and so…Either I go on the lam, but at my age you can understand that's not so easy, or else I go back home, and so I'm leaving tomorrow, on TAP, Rome-Lisbon, and then Lisbon-Accra…"

"But can you leave, it you don't have documents?"

"I have a passport, it's just expired. That's why I'm here in Rome, to renew it."

"Ah, you're in Rome?"

"Emiliano, believe me, I'm very sorry to leave the Maestro, but I have no choice…That's the way life is, everything changes in an instant, no? That's what Joan Didion says, too. Oh, I'm also sorry about the slap. I could see that you were upset, but sometimes a slap is useful…"

"I don't know, Mamadou. I don't think so. Not for me, that's for sure."

"But for me, yes. I've been on the receiving end lots of times. And they all did me good. But, sorry, just one thing, Emiliano…Can I ask you a question?"

"Sure."

"Okay, I leave tomorrow, and there's no way I can take with me all the books Vittorio has given me, because it would take a container, two even...But I can't live without books, and so, well, I wanted to know if it's true what you said at dinner the other night...that they're all on the internet..."

"Not everything. But a lot, yes...No, I mean, well, yeah, practically they're all there."

"And you can read them for free?"

"Sure."

"Without paying?"

"Yes."

"Really?"

"That's what the internet was created for."

"But how do you do it? Because, I'm not such an ace with the computer..."

"There are ways..."

"And can you teach them to me?"

"Sure."

"Ah, great. Then, thanks. Really, thanks a million. I'm so relieved. You've just taken a big weight off my heart, white brother. How can people live without books?"

"Badly, that's how...But how did he take the news, that you're leaving?"

"Ah, at first, not well...He got mad, wanted to go to the carabinieri and tell them he was the one who did the shooting, but then in the end he understood, and he even bought me a ticket in business class...He's a real friend, Vittorio, a great friend and a great maestro of life, and I will miss him a lot..."

"But why does he want to go to Milan?"

"I don't know, he didn't want to tell me. He says not to worry because it has nothing to do with his health. Look, Emiliano, I'm sure that when it comes down to it, he won't go, but if for some reason he really should go, you have to go there with him in every way, because he needs assistance."

"What kind of assistance?"

"First of all, he has no sense of direction. Then, sometimes he falls asleep at the wheel. And then he still has to take aspirin every day for his heart and his blood pressure pills right after breakfast and statins after dinner. He has medicines to take. Anyway, I've written it all out for you, you won't have any trouble. The pills are in the leather pouch inside the backpack, on the kitchen table. I also left you some nasal spray in case his nose gets stuffed up, because if his nose gets stuffed up, he thinks he's going to die, and he gets a panic attack...Make sure you get there early, before nine. He'll definitely still be in bed, go in the house and wait for him."

"Okay, where are the keys?"

"There aren't any keys. The house is always open...There's not one key in the whole house. One day he threw them all into the woods. He doesn't want the doors to be closed. No door, ever. He doesn't like closed doors, says it would seem like he was in prison. One time, a long time ago, he told me he always had to be ready to get away, but then he never went anywhere at all, poor Vittorio…"

He blew his nose.

"So good luck, and don't do anything stupid, seriously, because that guy is the nicest, kindest man, and most mixed up and…and devastated and brilliant and alone that there is, and I love him like a brother, no, even more than a brother, understand?"

His voice broke.

"Otherwise, I'll get on a plane and I'll come looking for you, damn it…"

I heard him start to cry and he hung up.

I looked up and my mother was still there in the doorway smiling.

"You're going to Milan together, right?"

"What?"

"I just heard it on television…"

"On television?"

"I'm so happy for you, Emiliano, so happy you wouldn't believe it. This is your big chance," she said, and went back to the kitchen.

I went to look at my profile on Instagram.

It had exploded.

According to Wikipedia

• • •

ACCORDING TO WIKIPEDIA the Archangel Gabriel is venerated by all three of the great monotheistic religions and has many names, including the Left Hand of God, the Angel of Death, the Great Ordainer, the Angel of Fire, the Integral, and the Messenger Angel.

It seems he's the celestial scribe, thus the patron saint of writers, and that he favors the ripening of fruit. It was he who directed the deluge of fire that the Lord decided to unleash on Sodom; he that announced to Mary that she would become the mother of Jesus; he who advised Joseph not to get angry with that poor woman who was to become the Sainted Virgin; and when, on Judgment Day, the loud blast of a horn is heard everywhere on Earth, the horn will be blown by Archangel Gabriel.

For me, on the other hand, he made my Instagram profile explode, because I went from forty followers to fifty thousand in just a few hours.

He had done a great job.

If you touched Vezzosi's picture on the piece in the *Corriere*, you opened my Instagram profile, now rebaptized @zapata97, where the picture of the two of us was posted accompanied by the comment *Vittorio and I* had set off on a *wild road trip in Italy* that we were going to document with pictures and videos, and it was going to last two days and two nights before ending up at the arena of the Milan Fair, Sunday morning, *at 12:00*, when the *Maestro* would be speaking about the eighties and nineties *to his female and male readers, but also to all of Italy, breaking twenty-five years of silence because he had something very important to say.*

There followed a *Stay tuned!* and a parade of hashtags, including #vittorioisback, #eighties, #zapata, #vezzosi, #zapataandvezzosi, #vittoriovezzosi, #picoftheday, #instagood, #wolvesinside, #wildtrip, #the80s, #milan, #milanfair, #surprise, #the90s, #twentyfiveyearslater, #newnovel, #event, #tellusvittoriotellus, #anothermasterpiece, #vezzosisuperstar, #nobodylikeu, #anchisessuperstar.

But that's not all.

Carlita Cosmay, the most followed influencer in Italy, whom I knew because Allegra often used to talk about her, had posted on all of her social profiles the picture of Vezzosi, and she had also posted a story about it on Instagram—a short video, later shared on Facebook and Twitter, in which she, white blouse and blue suit, hair pulled back, eyeglasses, was sitting at a glass-top desk with *The Wolves Inside* in her hands and saying that Vezzosi was not only a fantastic writer who had made us laugh and cry with this wonderful novel, but also *really and I mean really a handsome dude*, and that she would have been happy to do him, and then there appeared on the screen, in her handwriting, the script @zapata97 and the two hashtags that headed up the whole caravan that followed: #iwanttodovezzosi and #lastalphamale.

Carlita Cosmay had almost seven million followers, many of whom were not bots but real human beings, who adored her and followed her live and did everything she told them to do, like giving likes to anyone she wanted, following anyone who followed her, watching the movies and listening to the songs that she liked, and above all, buying everything that she said she personally used, from clothes to shoes, cosmetics, shampoo, costume jewelry, cell phones; an army of the faithful who, despite the splendor and luxury in which most of Carlita's posts showed her living (cabins of private airplanes, vacation resorts on exotic islands, wonderful houses with breathtaking views of the skylines of megacities all over the world, the jewels of a Persian empress, friendships with cinema and music superstars that she loved to host in her residences and that formed her audience as she cooked for them with an apron on, because Carlita loved to cook and was *bravissima*, so *brava* that if she had wanted to she could easily have become the chef of a Michelin-starred restaurant), were all convinced that she was nothing but a simple girl—a normal person just like they were normal, just a little prettier but not too much, endowed

with a brilliant mind, superfine taste, and a big heart, yes, but
still and always humble, most humble, and in need of friendship and affection and support because she had such a hard
life, really hard, and she had never forgotten who she was and
where she came from, and all the defeats and pain that she had
suffered, as demonstrated by those ingenious twilight posts
in which every now and again she was not afraid to show herself without makeup, disappointed, depressed, tired, sleepless,
even in tears, because, while she ruled the world and decided
the fates of the balance sheets of multinationals, Carlita was
a woman who suffered for love, seduced and abandoned by a
mysterious man with whom, even though he was a sleaze who
had left her alone with a child to raise, she was still so in love
that she refused to reveal his identity, letting it be known only
that he was someone very well-known and very married whose
family she did not want to ruin, and so she had renamed him
BiologicalDad and spoke to him only on Instagram, the only
place and system in which she felt strong enough, supported
as she was by her army of her faithful male and female followers, to manage to find the courage to write him certain public-
to-the-max messages that were really not all that bad, also and
above all because they varied with Carlita's moods, and during
the same day they could start sweet and turn sad, and from sad
turn furious, to then go back to sweet, and to these messages
the BiologicalDad—an asshole of the first order whose face
was not known but only his weight-lifter body—responded,
yes, but rarely, very rarely, as though he had so much else to do

in life besides respond to her, and was always blunt and often
contentious, and so loved and hated by Carlita's army, because
the mood of their goddess hung on the tone of his responses,
and though a sweet word from the BiologicalDad could light
up her day and make her so happy that her happiness spilled
over and infused the lives of her male and female followers,
his silence or, even worse, some wicked remark, could ruin
her day and consequently half of Italy's day, in which case Carlita's profile would be inundated with a deluge of little hearts
and kisses and clapping hands for which she always expressed
her gratitude, heartfelt but collective, without ever responding to anyone in particular; *in our hearts we are all equal,* and
responding to one or another would be to commit an injustice to millions of others, and create a disparity that would
lead to that negative spin mentioned by the Archangel, who
certainly deserved a lot of the credit for the wild success that
had made a millionairess of Carlita Cosmay, Friend to All and
the Divine, the Crying Saint and the Sassy Babe, the Mother
and the Lover, the Absolute Genius who had broken the bank
on the internet without knowing how to do a thing, and followed only two accounts: the one for the Louvre and the one
for Pope Francis.

Her #IwanttodoVezzosi shook Instagram down to its
foundations, and not only because Carlita had never used
that kind of language before, but especially because she had
never put any other man ahead of the BiologicalDad, not even
as a joke, and so as a furious debate broke out about whether

a man well over fifty like Vezzosi could ever be an answer to the cold insensitivity of the BiologicalDad, plus he was a writer…Fears were expressed that he, too, would take advantage, like all the other vicious males, of Carlita's goodness, but there were a lot among the faithful who believed, instead, that a man of culture would be the perfect companion for her, and that, because of his life experience, he would understand her and help her as never before.

But it was the BiologicalDad who brought the attention of the army of male and female followers to the salability of the product Vezzosi, which already risked being diluted in a sterile and noncommercial discussion.

In a rare post sent in from South Beach in Miami, the BiologicalDad was shown from behind, Kindle in hand, intent on getting a suntan, and he wrote that he had been rather hurt by the hashtag #IwanttodoVezzosi, and, for a second, he had even felt jealous, but then he had downloaded #wolvesinside and had started to read it, and had realized immediately that he absolutely could not compete with *the greatest Italian writer of all time.* At the bottom he included the usual cartload of hashtags, the link to my Instagram profile, and, a total novelty, the link to the Amazon page on *The Wolves Inside,* which, upon opening, revealed that Vezzosi's novel was once again racing triumphantly to the top of the bestsellers list.

The Last Great American Carburetor Engine

. . .

VEZZOSI BRUSHED A long lock of salt-and-pepper hair off his eyes, poked his glasses into position on his nose, pulled out of his pocket a transparent tube with the Kodak logo printed in relief, carefully pulled off the cap, and poured a heap of cocaine onto the CD jewel case that he had just asked me to keep *perfectly horizontal*.

"Tell me it doesn't smell like wild radicchio…"

As my heartbeat started to accelerate, I lifted the cover to my nose and smelled a pungent odor that I had never smelled before, and it actually smelled like a mixture of paint and, maybe, fresh-cut grass.

I nodded and started to hand the jewel case back to him, but Vezzosi stuck a hand into his jacket pocket, pulled out a wallet, took out a gray credit card—Diners Club, written in blue—and said:

"Hold it still."

He started to hit the cocaine with deft, rapid, chopping blows with the side of the card, and in a few seconds, he had eliminated every minimal thickness, transmuting it into a narrow rectangle of shiny white dust that he sliced into four equal lines.

"Go for it, Zapata."

I had slept very little and badly, after spending a lot of time reading the hundreds of comments from my new followers, among whom were major and minor rappers, deejays, fashion models, football players, influencers, actresses and actors, columnists, television emcees, and politicians from all sides, many of whom had also sent me private messages asking for *all-areas passes for the event*, and, as soon as I got to his house, I had found him standing next to the car with the engine running, raring to go, and I didn't even have time to open my mouth before we raced off, jolting down the mule path. After a few kilometers, he decided to stop in front of a big bar in a reconverted industrial warehouse because *it was time to have the breakfast of champions*, and he pulled out the cocaine and asked me if it smelled like wild radicchio.

Two carabinieri paused on their way out of the bar, blocking the closure of the automatic doors, which kept bolting back and forth in vain. They were talking about football with a customer. About the Florentine team, it seemed to me. Suddenly they turned to look at us, and came straight toward us. One of them looked to be around fifty, while the other was younger, more or less my age. Vezzosi handed me a banknote, rolled into a cylinder.

"Hurry up, come on."

They were about two steps away when I bent over the jewel case I was holding in my hand and said under my breath:

"Lord, forgive me and protect me, me and my weak and ill-considered life. Lord, light my way and keep watch over me always, even now, as I try my damnedest to ruin it in order to make it worth living…"

"Amen," Vezzosi responded, and I put the banknote at the head of the line and snorted, forcefully, and immediately felt the drug go all the way down to my throat and burn, and I had to squeeze my eyes shut and shake my head like a horse.

Vezzosi smiled, rolled down the window with two quick turns of the handle, and said to the carabinieri:

"Nice, isn't it?"

The older of the two had stuck his black-haired head just about into the car without so much as looking at me, as I quivered, motionless, my heartbeat pounding in my temples from fear, my right hand struggling to keep the jewel case on my lap without tilting it, and my left cupped over the coke that was still lying on it.

"But does it run on gas?" he asked, with an accent from the North, maybe Lombardy. Vezzosi started the engine and pumped the throttle. There was a roar, and the car bounced up and down on its suspensions.

"What do you think?"

"I told you so," said the carabiniere from the North to his partner. "It's a CJ-7. The Golden Eagle. V-8, 5000 cc. Three forward gears. A legendary machine. What is it, an '82?"

"'79. And, actually, this one is 6600 cc."

"A 401? Really? The legendary 401? The last great American carburetor engine?"

Vezzosi smiled with satisfaction.

"That's the one. I can see you know your engines..."

The carabiniere returned the smile.

"They are the legends of our time, no?"

"Would you like to try her?"

Taken by surprise, the carabiniere couldn't hold back a quick look toward his younger partner, as though he needed some kind of authorization from him, then he shook his head:

"Thanks, but I can't. I'm on duty."

Vezzosi gave it another shot of gas, and when the engine started humming with the old, hearty gurgle of the idle, it felt like I could hear the gasoline running through the pipes to fill up those eight cylinders, mix with air, burst into flame, and immediately turn into poisonous gas that streamed out of the exhaust pipe and spread all around us, as we serenely welcomed it into our lungs.

In the last few minutes, things had changed somewhat. My perceptions, I mean. My fear had gone away and been replaced by a sort of slow, warm, innocent good cheer, and now I was smiling, exhilarated by the discovery that in the few magical centimeters of the intersection between nose, throat, and brain, there had begun to spread a sense of elemental bitterness and cold that I had never felt before, but that I found intensely pleasant.

"Ah come on, at least take a spin around the parking lot."

Yes, because in front of the bar-warehouse there was a parking lot so big it deserved its own place name—they had given it the name of one of the lesser-known mafia victims—and at one time it was where trucks loaded and unloaded goods for the four small businesses that lined one side of it, now all closed down.

The carabiniere from the North hesitated, but Vezzosi jumped out of the Jeep to leave him the driver's seat and I remained, horrified, in the passenger's seat, the jewel case with the coke in my hand, looking at that fifty-year-old carabiniere, who, incredibly, handed his cap to his partner, climbed in, adjusted the seat and the mirror, pumped the gas pedal, shifted into first, and took off, pedal to the metal, with a deafening roar.

The hood popped up as if the Jeep were about to do a wheelie, and he kept on saying *Fuck, fuck,* and in no time, we were at the end of the lot and screeched to a stop just a few centimeters from the rollup door of one of the shut-down shops. CITARELLA CONSTRUCTION was written on it.

I couldn't find the courage to look and see what had happened to the jewel case. The carabiniere shifted into reverse and turned the Jeep around to head back, he slammed on the gas again and peeled out even faster than before, if possible, and this time I would have sworn that the front wheels had actually come off the ground, and in an instant we were again in front of Vezzosi and the young carabiniere, who was looking around nervously, because there was not one customer in the bar who had not come out to see the show.

The carabiniere from the North got out of the Jeep. Then he asked Vezzosi, in a loud voice:

"The modification is recorded on the registration, right?"

"Sure. Would you like to see it?"

He smiled.

"No, that's all right. I trust you. You can go."

He winked and, as they were shaking hands, the carabiniere whispered:

"Thanks a million, Vezzosi. Mother Mary, for a minute there, I was a kid again…"

Vezzosi smiled, got back in the Jeep, and gave them a short wave good-bye, then turned to look at me as I continued to keep my cupped hand over the jewel case and the lines of coke that were maybe, or maybe not, still there, and he burst out laughing. That rankled me and I said:

"There's nothing to laugh about, you know? And after breakfast you've got to take your blood pressure pills and the aspirin…"

His laugh turned into a roar.

"Plus, you know how much a car like this pollutes?"

And he, tears in his eyes from laughing so hard:

"Ah, go fuck yourself, Zapata, we're out of here…"

He put it into first and pulled out, then he accelerated, and the rumble of the last great American carburetor engine grew into a crescendo that filled the parking lot, the road, and the entire world.

Bikini

. . .

WHEN WE GOT within range of the toll booth at the entrance to the highway, Vezzosi pulled over and stopped the Jeep next to a rusty guardrail that, instead of keeping cars from driving off the road, looked like it was there to block the advance onto the roadway of an immense, abandoned palm grove, whose expansion had first covered and then swallowed the sign of the nursery—FROSINI LUCIANO AND SONS—that had planted it years ago.

He asked me for the jewel case and, after reconstructing the lines of the coke that I had miraculously managed to keep from spilling in all the tumult, he snorted all three, one after the other, calmly, composed, without any grimaces or even clearing his throat, *professionally*, while I looked at him and smiled at the idea that I was supposed to be the one taking care of him.

I, who was sitting next to him in his forty-year-old car, incapable of doing anything but sit there, immobile, enjoying the cocaine that I had not had the courage to refuse and that was now invading my body and spirit, making my heart dance in my chest and etching an idiotic smile on my boyish face. I, who had never used it or even known anyone who had, and who hadn't ever even smoked a joint, because doing drugs had always seemed to me a sign of weakness and desperation, plus when I was fourteen I had promised my dad that I would not do drugs, any drug, ever. I, however, who had no desire at all to think about it, about all those things, not on that superb end-of-May morning, with the sun shining in a clear, big sky, blue as the team jersey of Uruguay.

"Now we open the car," Vezzosi said, after taking a deep breath and exhaling a long puff of satisfaction.

"What?"

"Everything comes off. Starting with the bikini."

Still seated, he detached the cotton cloth that was protecting our heads from the sun, rolled it up, and threw it on the back seat.

"That was the bikini."

He jumped out of the Jeep and looked it over for a few seconds.

"Off with the doors, too."

"The doors?"

He took hold of the door on the driver's side, which was still open, lifted it off the hinges, and there it was, in his hands.

"You mean, that's all that was holding it on, Vezzosi? Is that allowed?"

He leaned it up against the guardrail, walked around the car, opened the door on my side, lifted it off the hinges, and laid it over the other. Then he took another look at the car.

"I'll tell you something else, Zapata, the windshield is coming off, too."

"What?" I said again. I was clueless.

"In this car, you can lower it, and you know why? Because the Jeep was built as a war vehicle, and the reflection of the sunlight would make it a target for snipers, so..."

He got back in the driver's seat and started rummaging around near the steering wheel.

"Come on, unscrew your side too."

He pointed out a big plastic handle at the end of the dashboard. I unscrewed it easily, until it came off in my hand.

"And now?"

"Now, let's lower it."

He started pushing the windshield forward, and I did the same. It was hard, but it gave way almost immediately with a short groan, and we laid it on the hood, to which Vezzosi secured it, using the two little hooks on the sides of the decal of the big bronze eagle.

I couldn't help but smile.

"But it's prettier like this, all naked! It's a whole lot prettier, really, plus they won't shoot at us anymore."

Vezzosi bent over to look behind his seat, opened up a little portable refrigerator, and pulled out a bottle and two crystal wineglasses that he handed to me. He uncorked the bottle and filled them with white wine.

"A toast, Zapata!" he announced, raising his glass, "To our journey!"

We guzzled that marvelous wine in a single gulp—the same wine that we had drunk at dinner—and Vezzosi proceeded to fill our glasses again. I realized that I would need another sense to be able to describe the tastes and aromas that it unleashed in my mouth. It seemed to me I could taste the aroma of broom flowers...But how do broom flowers make it into wine?

"So, are we off to Milan?"

He glared at me.

"Who told you that? Who talked, damn it?"

"What do you mean, who talked? Everyone's talking about it. It's on the net. The world knows it."

He huffed.

"The world...Why doesn't the world mind its own fucking business, huh?"

"Are you really going to speak to all those people?"

"I think so, but I'm not sure. Maybe. We'll see. But why did you say *all those people*? How many are there going to be?"

Only then did I realize that he knew nothing. *He doesn't read the newspapers. He doesn't use the internet. Zero.* He thought he was going to be speaking to a couple dozen exhibitors.

"I don't know." I tried to recover. "I imagine there'll be quite a few...Listen, can I tell Allegra?"

"Who's Allegra?"

"The woman of my life, Maestro Vezzosi? She's an admirer of yours."

"Ah, the women of our lives...Serious stuff, that. At this point, though, I'd say we can use the informal *tu*, Zapata."

"Thanks, but I'm not sure I can manage it."

"Tell her to come, why not?"

"But if I tell her, there'll be no way to hold her back and she'll do anything she can to come to Milan, and so you're going to speak, right? We're not going to have her come for nothing, are we?"

Vezzosi opened his arms out wide, looked up at the sky.

"*Quién sabe*, Zapata? We'll have to see how I'm feeling that morning, now I can't make any commitments for tomorrow. I might even be dead, tomorrow, and you, too...Look, let's do this: we leave now in our marvelous Jeep and we have a glorious trip. We drink and do drugs all day long. We stop and have lunch in Bologna, take all the time we want. Serenity. Total serenity. Then we get back on the road, and at eight o'clock, we arrive in Milan, where we have a very important dinner date. We sleep there, and tomorrow we decide whether to speak or not, because we don't give a shit about crowds, and then, however it goes, we get back in the car and go home. Okay? Are we agreed?"

He waited for my answer, as though he needed my approval to go on: as if, in order to set out on his glorious journey, he needed me, who only a few days ago had sat down at his table and called him a fake and Mr. Magoo and a fraud and piece of shit.

"We drink and do drugs all day, Vezzosi? Me, too?"

"Naturally. And this Allegra, I want to meet her. Have her come."

He refilled the glasses.

"Come on, then we'll put it back in the fridge."

We drank in big gulps, and it seemed to me that in that marvelous wine there was also the taste of the stones I used to put in my mouth as a kid, but I didn't have the courage to tell Vezzosi, who in the meantime was fishing out of the back seat a jeans jacket with a fur lining that he put on right away, and then he gave me a beige bush jacket with a NASA patch.

"Treat it well, it's an original jacket. Romano said he bought it contraband, at Camp Darby in Livorno, from a marine from Oklahoma."

"Who's Romano?"

"A wild man…Just think that in '76, when he was sixteen, he was in Florida to play in the Orange Bowl Tennis Championship, which, by the way, he won, but after the semifinal he slipped away and went to Cape Canaveral because he wanted to see NASA, and the police looked for him all over Florida before they found him there, sitting on the ground outside the museum, with a dreamy look on his face, still dressed in his tennis outfit, holding an Apollo 11 T-shirt and that badge there in his pants pocket…He also went off to join the French Foreign Legion, Romano, but then he came back after two weeks…"

"Huh? Where did he go?"

"He was my fucking idol…"

He opened the glove compartment and pulled out a pair of black sunglasses.

"Here, Zapata. Put these on. They're Wayfarers. The only possible sunglasses."

He turned on the engine, which started growling like a beast.

"Wait, Vezzosi, the doors? Where do they go?"

We got out of the car and looked around.

"Let's hide them here, under Frosini's palm trees."

"What?"

"What, are you deaf? All you say is *what, what...*"

"No, sorry... It's just a habit..."

"Get rid of it. It's irritating. Come on, let's go."

He grabbed one of the doors, climbed over the guardrail, took a few steps into that wild palm grove, and leaned it up against an enormous trunk, and I did the same.

"They're very strange, aren't they though, Vezzosi, these car doors leaning against the palm trees?"

"You're right, they're incredibly strange."

We kept on looking at them.

"Who knows if anyone else has ever done this in the entire history of the world, this thing of leaning car doors against palm trees..."

He shrugged his shoulders.

"Anyhow, tomorrow we're coming back to get them. Let's go, Zapata!"

We got back in the Jeep and started off, and Vezzosi crossed all the entering lanes to take the ticket from the live hands of the tollbooth operator and not from the slit on the front of a machine. They said good-bye to each other.

"Oh, you know him?"

"No, but we're both humans. It's only right to say hello and good-bye."

An audiocassette appeared in his hand, and he put it into the slit in the stereo right in the center of the Jeep's big dashboard, in front of the stick. He pumped up the volume to the max and, between clicks and whishing sounds, said:

"This disc was played for us by that guy from Discs and More, must be forty years ago now, for me and Fede... It was in the morning, we had blown off school, and we were electrified, Zapata, I mean electrified, and then we bought it and raced right home on our souped-up Vespas, in the pouring rain, to copy it onto two cassettes that we then gave to the two girls with whom we were deliriously in love. In vain, by the way, if I remember correctly..."

And then the tape started to play a song that I recognized immediately because I had heard it a thousand times without even taking note of it... In elevators, supermarkets, shopping centers, even in movies, but this time it was totally different. It could have been the coke, or the wine, or both together, but every note hit me, touched me inside, and I had to close my eyes to better follow its slow unfolding of those guitar chords that was so sweet and mellow that it seemed like a caress— *dad's caress*, I thought—and when the singer started to sing about the empty highway and the cool wind in his hair, there, I had to open them again because it was exactly everything that I was feeling and seeing in that moment, and it was as though

I were living inside that marvelous song that was about a hotel in California, if I understood correctly. Then suddenly something unwound in my chest and I started to cry, who knows why, and I couldn't get myself to stop, and when he noticed, Vezzosi shouted into the blustery wind:

"Bravo, Zapata, cry! It'll do you so much good."

Like Riding a Scooter

• • •

PRACTICALLY, IT WAS like riding a scooter.

The wind was right in my face, together with the dust and the exhaust fumes and the insects and stones shooting up behind the trucks, and it was really uncomfortable, so uncomfortable that at first it seemed impossible to me to drive for three hundred kilometers in those conditions, and at one point I was just about to tell Vezzosi to stop, but he seemed so happy to be driving and jabbering away and singing the songs that followed one another on the stereo that I didn't. Instead, I closed my eyes, and after a while I started to relax in all of that blowing around, the sound of the engine stopped pounding in my ears, and I was almost starting to let myself go, and in the end I liked that feeling of being totally at the mercy of events, exposed to any outcome, defenseless and certainly bound to die in any accident because, in addition to the windshield, and the top, and the doors, the Jeep also had no seat belts.

"I cut them," Vezzosi had explained, "they were breaking my balls."

Passini called me constantly, but I didn't answer, and I had sent a message to Allegra with the big news, and she had called me back right away, but I didn't answer her call either because I didn't feel like talking to her in front of Vezzosi, plus there was too much wind and I wouldn't have understood anything, and so then she sent me a message with a long series of little differently colored hearts and exclamation points, and assured me that she would be arriving in Milan early in the morning.

Everything was fine, in other words.

The toasts kept coming and we finished the wine, the jackets were old but they protected us from the wind, and the only possible sunglasses protected our eyes as we climbed, at no more than ninety kilometers an hour, up the Apennines that were parading by, arid and majestic, and I forced myself to think that what had only just begun was not a simple journey, but the first leg of a sort of apprenticeship, maybe even a *cursus honorum*.

When we got to the dividing point, Vezzosi blew off the direct lanes and chose the older, panoramic route, and I, who had never taken either, asked him what the difference was.

"The direct lanes are a newly built road that bores through the mountains and you're practically always going straight, while the panoramic, on the other hand, is the fucked-up name they gave to the old Florence-Bologna highway that I've driven a thousand times and know by heart... Practically, it was a kind of Russian roulette because there wasn't a trip where you didn't risk your life at least once along the way…"

He shook his head, laughing.

"It was hell, Zapata, you had to pay attention to everything…the killer trucks, the terrified drivers, the bald tires and the drum brakes that everybody had, the passes that you always made because back then there was no way you were going to waste time behind someone who drove slow, the curves that narrowed without warning, the uneven asphalt, the potholes, the ruts, the road repairs that never seemed to finish, the sudden bottlenecks at the end of the curves, the deviations down to one-lane traffic, the vehicles stopped in the emergency lane and the ones stopped in the middle of the road, the fatal accidents that caused other fatal accidents, the multicar bang-ups, the races against other cars because everybody had the throttle to the floor, always and rightly…The drivers who didn't know how to drive and the ones who thought they did; the ones who tailgated and high-beamed you when you couldn't change lanes even if you wanted to, and so you gave them the finger, and one time out of three you had to stop at the service area to explain yourself better with a few smacks upside the head…And then the fog, rain, snow, wind, ice, hail, oil slicks, tire treads left by trucks, those fucking aerodynamic mud flaps that fell off the fucking trucks…The sun that blinded you when you came out of the tunnels, the tunnels, the music that was always in your ears, Fede's endless whining about women, always about women, to the screaming fights that always and only broke out when the two of us, Fede and I, were in the car together, the fantasizing about present, past, and future, and when I suddenly started crying and kept on driving all the same even if I couldn't see a thing..."

"Who is Fede?" I asked, but Vezzosi didn't answer and remained quiet for a while as we continued to climb on that highway that, going as slow as we were, didn't seem so dangerous, on the contrary, because the curves were gentle and the lanes were wide and ample, and I thought that maybe they had designed and built it, the Florence-Bologna, just so it would be traveled at our snail-like pace, but I didn't tell him that.

As alone as we were on that big strip of blanched asphalt, if not for some rare trucks loaded with lumber, we had all the time we needed to look around and admire the beauty of the wild valleys.

"You see, Zapata, man has withdrawn from those valleys, and now they're populated by boar as big as donkeys and wolves as ferocious as lions, and their mortal battles shake the centuries-old oaks... They say that falcons live there, and eagles," he announced as he waved at the mammoth old eighteen-wheelers that passed us in slow motion, their engines revving, spitting black carcinogenic smoke and blowing their bi-toned horns, and it wasn't easy to understand if they were saluting us or telling us to shove it up our ass, me and Vezzosi, who, as soon as we passed the peak at Roncobilaccio, decided it was time to try to snort cocaine while he was driving, but we discovered that with the windshield down it wasn't possible, and so we spread a few decigrams out on the highway and Vezzosi said that we had performed an apotropaic ritual.

Osteria Italiana

. . .

WHEN WE GOT to Bologna we got off the highway because he wanted to take me to lunch in a *fantastic osteria*, and then *get ourselves a tattoo*.

"I'm not getting a damn tattoo."

"Why not?"

"Because, no. I don't like them and I never have."

"You're afraid of needles."

"Not true."

"But yes."

"Yes, all right, I'm afraid of needles. And so?"

"You're a wimp, Zapata."

"What if I were?"

We proceeded to get lost among the boulevards of that gorgeous city and went spinning around like tops for a long time, until Vezzosi got fed up and parked the Jeep in a "no parking" place, and we started off on what became an endless trek along the porticoed sidewalks.

"Oh, not even once have I not gotten lost in this city, shit..."

In the end we happened on the osteria. On the door's glass panel was written in gothic letters OSTERIA ITALIANA. Vezzosi said he wasn't sure he remembered the name but that certainly wasn't it.

"And what's with the fucking gothic lettering?"

"So what do we do, Vezzosi?"

"As long as it's taken us to get here, we might as well go in..."

We went in, and it was empty. We were greeted immediately by a robust forty-year-old, with a black Lacoste and a shaved head and an ambitious hint of sideburns that ended brusquely at half-cheek, as though they hadn't had the courage to go any farther. He gestured to us to sit at a corner table and went into the kitchen without saying a word. It seemed like he was in a bad mood. I was a little afraid of him.

"Looks like they must be under new management, Zapata. It used to be one of those classic old Bolognese osterias, you know? Funky, noisy, really Bolognese, always lively...Food was fantastic...lasagna, tortellini. I'm ready to chow down, Zapata, how about you?"

Behind Vezzosi, there was a bust of the Duce, on a sort of pedestal, between two tables. I got up and went over to take a look at it. It was made of black plastic, all shiny, and on the walls, forming a kind of crown, were two posters, framed and dated from the early seventies, covered with gothic crosses, and announcing get-togethers, called Hobbit Camps, in small, backwater places in central and southern Italy. I pointed them out to Vezzosi and he came over to look.

"Well, what do you know... I had heard about these posters, but I'd never seen one... In those years, it was rare that they lasted for more than a few hours plastered on walls around the city..."

The shaved head came back in the room, huffing, and said that the cook was on vacation and all they had was tagliatelle with meat sauce and stew. And some mortadella. Vezzosi was irked.

"What? That's it? Excuse me, but what happened? Everything is different... What happened to the gentleman with the beard, fat, friendly, who was a friend of Dante Canè... What was his name?"

The shaved head shook no.

"But yeah, and his son, the sommelier... Really smart kid, lots of fun, knew all of the Bourgognes..."

The shaved head kept shaking. Then said:

"They're gone. New management. So, what do you want to order?"

Vezzosi stared at him.

"You know what? I lost my appetite."

"Me, too," I said, in an outburst of courage that I didn't know I had.

After a moment of silence, Vezzosi opened up.

"And anyway, this thing that Tolkien was one of yours is really enough to make a guy die laughing, I mean, really... It's so damn Italian, no one in the rest of the world claims that. You don't understand a damn thing about *The Lord of the Rings*...Hobbit Camps...Have you even read the book, I mean, even once, huh? And the film? Have you ever seen the film? Even that would be enough...You tell me what the fuck Tolkien had to do with you Fascists..."

The shaved head was surprised. He kept on switching his gaze between me and Vezzosi, as though he were trying to figure out who we were and what we wanted.

"He was one of us," he said, "sure he was."

"One of you, my ass," Vezzosi shot back. "He was a conservative, Tolkien, not a reactionary. There's a big difference. You know that? Plus, in any case, you people don't belong to the Shire...If anything, you belong to the ogres, and not even to the Uruk-hai, who in the end at least had a little dignity...You're those cutthroat monsters, all contorted, always famished, born of the obscene and unspeakable couplings of corrupt elves and animals..."

The shaved head retreated a step, as though pushed by Vezzosi's words.

"It's all Zolla's fault for that fucking introduction that hardly does anything except recount the plot of the book, like the two-bit reviewers who don't know what else to write...I imagine one of yours who knew how to read got an eyeful of that stuff and went running to you, who were hitting each other with chains in some back alley, and told you, *Oh, guys, hold up a minute, Tolkien's a Fascist like us, but he can't say so because of the worldwide conspiracy of Jews and Communists, and so he resorts to metaphors, understand?* And all of you, in chorus, *What the fuck's a metaphor?*

He couldn't help smiling at his own joke.

"Anyway, that whole story is a bunch of bullshit, you understand? And even today, there's got to be some difference between what's true and what's not, damn it! If Mamadou were here, you'd be in trouble... He would send you all to the Hobbit Camps..."

Vezzosi had raised his voice, and an old Pakistani guy stuck his head out of the door to the kitchen, but as soon as he saw us, he retreated back in. The shaved head's eyebrows were still wrinkled. He wasn't afraid, naturally, but he seemed to be calculating whether it was worth punching out an overweight old guy and a young kid in his restaurant, for a literary dispute. Then he decided.

"Look, then, let's do this. You two get the hell out of my restaurant and you..." He pointed to me. "You take him to the rest home, give him his medicine, and put him to bed, and this whole story ends here and now and I don't call the carabinieri, okay?"

"Rest home? The carabinieri? What the fuck are you saying? If the carabinieri come, they'll arrest you and close the place," Vezzosi shouted. "You sure as hell can't keep a bust of Mussolini in your restaurant and all of those posters... And what the hell do the gothic crosses have to do with you, anyway? Nothing, not even those! They're druid symbols. You stole them! Goddam thieves! And get rid of the fucking swastika you've got around your neck, shithead!"

I just got a glimpse of it. It was a small gold swastika swinging at the end of a chain, in the middle of his chest hair that seemed to sprout directly from the shaved head's neck.

"Eh no! Eh no, fucking shit!" he started screaming, too, revealing a shrill and almost feminine voice that must have been set off by all the agitation and clashed with his look and must surely have been the object of scorn in his life—the defect for which he was always made fun of by his friends and maybe also the main reason why he had gone and shut himself inside an osteria that he obviously didn't know how to run, just so he could have a place where he, and only he, could be in command, and no one pulled his chain, and Mussolini was still living.

"You're the shithead, old man! This is my place, and in my place, I do whatever the fuck I want, understand? And if I want to keep the Duce in my restaurant, I keep him! And if I want to keep a swastika around my neck, I keep it, understand? We're still free, in Italy! There's freedom of expression! I'm free to say what I want, got it? And you've got to respect it, my freedom, you got that, you old lunatic?"

About that, you got to admit, he was right: Vezzosi was acting like a lunatic. His arms raised to the heavens, his vocal cords bulging in his neck, he was screaming:

"My God, what I have to listen to! A Fascist claiming his freedom of expression! How the hell did we get to this point, eh? Let's get out of here, Zapata! Out of this filthy stinking pigsty!"

He jerked his body around, gave a healthy kick to one of the chairs, and exited the osteria, and in order to catch up with him I had to quicken my step, almost running. Almost immediately, I was gasping for breath. How long had it been since I had run! When I caught up to him, he stopped and looked at me.

"What the fuck has happened to Italy, huh? Tell me what happened!"

I shrugged my shoulders, and he headed off, with long strides, through the porticoes, cursing under his breath at God and the Madonna.

And I:

"Hey, no blasphemy, Vezzosi!"

Simon & Garfunkel

• • •

HE DIDN'T CALM down until I pointed out to him a *salmoneria*.

He had to smile over the fact that there existed a place with a name like that, but once we were inside, he very much appreciated that, in addition to salmon, you could also order sandwiches with herring, sturgeon, mackerel, and halibut from Greenland, whatever that was. He ordered one of each fish and perched on a stool at the counter, monitoring their preparation, and he never stopped talking:

"These days, inventing names is an underground operation, but what time is it? Ah, look, our Mamadou has just left...I'm going to miss him a lot, that piece of work...As a kid, he was a boxer, and he even fought Azumah Nelson when he was still an amateur...Here, Zapata, taste how good this Balik is, with all the drugs you've been doing and will be doing, you've got to eat something...Look, let's get this golden Grecanico from Aetna, thanks...You know how we met, me and Mamadou? One night, at the Yab, he saved me…The book had just come out, and I was really hot, you know, and I had been drinking, and, well, I got into a spat with three young lads and things got a little chancy, and up comes this Black fireplug with eyes like live coals…And he didn't say a word, he sat down next to me and they scampered out of there like fawns…And you know why he came over? Because he'd recognized me…He had read the book…Long story short, we became friends, but then he ended up in some pretty ugly circles, and one morning I had to go pick him up, literally, at a playground for kids, under a merry-go-round, half-dead like White Fang. They'd broken his arms and legs with clubs…Oh, he was on his way out…No, not by the glass, what are you talking about, by the glass…Do we perhaps look like people who drink by the glass, Professor De Vito and myself? The bottle, the whole bottle…Excuse me, young man, is this marvelous fillet perhaps the Czar Nikolaj cut? No? Because it seemed a little…it's good, though, very good…My compliments, truly…Where was I? Ah, yes, I had him operated on and brought him to my house for months, while he was convalescing, and when he was better, he asked me if he could stay and be a sort of factotum, and since that day he started reading ravenously. Oh, Zapata, I've never seen a man read like that. He didn't even sleep, so he could keep on reading. He started with history, and immediately lost his head over Lorenzo de' Medici…spent entire afternoons walking the streets of Florence to see where the Magnificent had walked…Then he moved on to philosophy…By the way, he read your thesis and really liked it, did he tell you? But his true love was literature. He just reveled in it…laughed, cried, woke me up at night to talk about Tolstoy and Dostoyevsky…And then he fell in love with the Americans, especially Fitzgerald, but *The Sun Also Rises* he liked a lot, too…And then he got on to Salinger, Carver, and Denis Johnson…His latest was Joan Didion…All told, over the years, the guy got himself a first-class education. He writes, too, but poetry, and it's tough to write poetry, and he's just so refined…Great translator, by the way. Did he tell you he translates for Mondadori under a false name?"

When we were back out strolling under the porticoes, I stayed a few meters behind him, and as we walked along in silence, I checked my telephone. There were a bunch of messages and unanswered calls from numbers not in my contacts. My mother told me again that they were still talking about us on television and still showing our picture, and she was so proud of me.

Passini asked if we had left and where were the other pictures and videos because they had told him they needed them right away. The Archangel had sent me a picture of a press release from the fair announcing the advance sale of *ten thousand* tickets, and, underneath the picture, a laughing face and a black heart. Allegra wrote that she had seen me on TV and that she was very, very glad to be coming tomorrow. Monnanni announced that we were the modern-day Argonauts, Vezzosi and I, and that he would have given his right arm to be able to be with us.

On Instagram, I was up to *seventy thousand* followers, in part because Carlita had posted another story, where she waved around an *all-areas-pass* for the Vezzosi event and winked as the script @zapata97 appeared on the screen, and said that by now the Sunday morning event had become the happening of the season, forget Springsteen, forget Vasco Rossi…

"Zapata, come on, we're there!"

I looked up and saw Vezzosi going in through the glass door of what looked like a doctor's office, only the sign on it said ARIES, and I had never seen doctors' offices where music was blasting and patients were welcomed by a girl with tattoos on her arms and neck who started hugging and kissing Vezzosi, calling him Maestro over and over again. Then the tattoo artist arrived, a skinny guy with sparkling eyes and a well-trimmed beard and a gold earring. He must have been around fifty but seemed like a kid, and he and Vezzosi embraced silently for a long time.

When they released from the embrace, the tattoo artist was teary-eyed.

"So great to see you here again, Vezzosi, fuckin' a! What an honor…"

"Well, if the mountain doesn't go to Mohammed…"

"Ah, come on, what mountain… I've been coming to your house to tattoo you for twenty years… Who's this?"

"My friend Zapata. A real Communist, hard-core, with steel balls, but he's got his defects, too… This is his first tattoo, and he wants to write on his chest the name of his lost lady, Alice..."

"Allegra," I heard myself say. *Communist? Hard-core? Steel balls?*

"Sure, okay, whatever her name is...I, on the other hand, want to do another script, but I still haven't chosen the font. Let's go choose it, our girlfriend here can take care of Zapata..."

Vezzosi put an arm on the shoulder of the tattoo artist and they disappeared behind an accordion door while I tried to find the right words to explain that I was absolutely not a Communist and I didn't have steel balls and wasn't the least bit interested in having them. The girlfriend tattoo artist—a slender twenty-five-year-old, with ivory skin, short, double-cut jet-black hair, and piercings all over—took me under her arm and asked why Alice had left me, seeing as I was such a well-mannered boy, and meanwhile she led me into a side room with gypsum board walls on which were hanging dozens of drawings of dragons and flowers and birds and monstrously muscular warriors.

She ordered me to sit down on a sort of dentist's chair and asked which font I wanted, and I replied that I didn't want to be tattooed: that was just Vezzosi's bullshit.

"No? Why not? It's a beautiful thing, a wonderful present you're giving her. If only I had someone who would tattoo my name on his heart..."

I had never thought that the tattoo wasn't for me but for Allegra.

"Really, you'd like that?"

"Sure, of course…It works, I'm telling you, especially if we find a nice font. You can even write it with your own handwriting if you want. *Alice*. Come on, try it, let's see how it goes…"

She handed me paper and pen and stood there looking at me, and I smiled and shook my head, but started to think it was indeed possible, that crazy idea to make me write Allegra's name on my heart, and so I wrote it out, simply, in block letters, like I used to write it when we were in school during math class and I would give her a tap with my elbow and show it to her and she would whisper to me *What the fuck does that mean*, and I would smile because I knew damn well what it meant.

I handed the paper to the tattoo artist, but she was involved in some complicated preparatory operations with a menacing-looking sort of metallic drill-pen, and a minute went by before she looked at it.

"*Allegra?* But wasn't it Alice? Mistakes aren't allowed…"

"Allegra, damn it!" I said again, and she started laughing and recopied the script onto a special paper and asked me where I wanted it, and I said I wanted it on my chest, to the left, just over my heart, and then she ordered me to take off my T-shirt and when I asked if I could just raise it, she said no, that I had to take it off, and so I did.

It was blue, one of those with a collar, and on the front, it had the yellow logo of a sportswear company that had gone bankrupt in the nineties, and I was little ashamed of it, but nothing compared to how ashamed I was of my torso with my ribs poking out and my paunch, which, looking at it reflected in the mirror, managed to appear both skinny and chubby at the same time, and anyway, utterly graceless.

Because that was an intimate situation, no doubt about it. Very intimate, and very embarrassing. I had never been in such intimacy—half-naked, shut inside a room—with a girl other than Allegra or, God forgive me, that one without a name doing the lap dance the other night, and as the tattoo artist turned to get the tissue paper, I took a sniff of both of my armpits to be sure they wouldn't betray me.

She applied the tissue paper to my chest, gave me a mirror, and there it was, the script ALLEGRA on my heart. It was perfect, and true, and I loved it. I told her it was fine, she asked me if she could begin, and I answered yes, and then she slipped her hands into some transparent latex gloves. When the metallic pen started to buzz, I asked her if it was going to hurt.

"A lot, no. But a little, yes. Come on, it's normal, but no big deal...But no, come on, why are you getting so pale?...What, do you want to stop? There's no problem if you want to stop, really, just don't faint on me, okay? Once a big, tall guy fainted on me, and we had to call an ambulance..."

I couldn't stand it, this thing of always being so up front.

"What do you mean, pale? I've got fair skin, that's all. Go right ahead..."

"Are you sure?"

"Yes."

She began, and it did actually hurt a little, sure, and at one point I had to grit my teeth, but then I realized that it was more for fear than for pain, and anyway it was better if I didn't look, and so I closed my eyes and didn't reopen them until my phone started ringing.

I gestured to the tattoo artist, and she stopped. It was my mother, I had to answer. Ever since the day she had called me to tell me about my dad, every call of hers startled me: every time I was afraid that, instead of her voice, I was going to hear the voice of a police officer or a doctor, who would introduce himself and then tell me that something irreparable had happened.

"Emiliano! I'm overwhelmed, I'm so happy for you!"

"What happened, Mama?"

"Are you already in Milan?"

"No, we stopped in Bologna for lunch."

"Oh, good. Smart idea. Because in Milan, they're all expecting you, you know? All the shows are talking about it, they say it's going to be a very important event and that people are coming from all over Italy to hear him, because he's supposed to say some very important things, Vezzosi, even more than Celentano... They say it's going to be a beautiful speech, that will point the way for those like us who have missed out on everything..."

"What are you talking about, Mama?"

"I'm not saying it, it's what they're saying on TV. But I think it's true. No, I know that it's true. Have you already read it, the speech? Is it nice? What does it say? Can you tell me about it? I won't tell anybody…"

"No, there isn't any speech."

"But there will be…Everybody's waiting for it…"

"Everybody who?"

"They've been interviewing people my age on the streets, but even younger people, too, and everyone's saying they're expecting a lot from him, in these dark times…A ray of light. Some hope."

"You've got to be kidding, Mama…"

"No, why would I kid you…It's such a beautiful thing, Emiliano! The entire nation is looking to him, like Joe DiMaggio in that fantastic song by Simon and Garfunkel, I wonder if you know it…Your father loved Simon and Garfunkel, we always used to listen to them in the car when we went to the beach, before you were born…Ah, Emiliano, my little boy, you don't know what I would give to come along with you…I would like so much to hear someone tell about the beautiful things from our past…"

"Mama, that's not a good idea, believe me."

"I know, I know…I'm not coming, don't worry. I don't want to bother you…"

"But no, you're not bothering me."

"It doesn't matter, Emiliano, if you're there, it's as if I were there. But make sure you cherish every moment. It's a wonderful experience for you. Anyway, they're going to broadcast it live, so I'll be able to see it anyway…"

"What do you mean, live?"

"Yes, tomorrow at noon, on television. I'm really hoping to see you, too … But now I'll get off, I don't want to bother you. We'll talk later. Maybe later you can let me talk to him, okay?"

"Sure, Mama."

"That would be so nice. It would be an honor."

"Sure, Mama. Right now, I can't, but later on I'll let you talk to him."

"Wonderful. Thanks. I can't wait. So, good-bye for now, and congratulations!"

And she hung up.

"Your mother is a real fan of Vittorio's, huh? Mine, too … I'm ready to start again, okay?"

It didn't take her long to finish, not long at all, and in no time I had the mirror in hand and there it was, the script AL-LEGRA tattooed on my chest. I smiled.

I was different, there was no doubt. Something had happened, and I was changed forever. I would no longer be the same person who had entered that place a half hour ago, even if I'd wanted to be. I had been *marked*, I had said good-bye to something that I really didn't know very well what it was, if not an infantile idea of cleanliness, an unwanted and child-like whiteness that was bound to be dirtied anyway, sooner or later, in one way or another.

"Did I do a good job?"

"Fantastic."

She rubbed some Vaseline on the script and she covered it with transparent plastic, then furrowed her brow in an imitation of a sad frown.

"There's something else we should do, Emiliano... Shall we take off this little beard?? You'd look so much better without it..."

"You think so?"

"Definitely... It'll only take me a second..."

She bent over me, and she had a clean smell that was so wonderful. I closed my eyes and heard her using first the scissors, then shaving cream and razor.

"Now you can reopen them," she said, and I saw myself clean shaven in the mirror. I looked like a giant baby, and smiled. She said I looked better, much better, and added that she was really sorry she couldn't come to Milan.

"I'm really worried about Vittorio, you know? He must be under tremendous tension about speaking to an audience, all the hype that has been unleashed around it is the farthest thing from him I can imagine, and it scares me, to tell you the truth, scares me a lot, because he is the most delicate person in the world, I mean in absolute terms... He gets hurt by everything, even rose petals... But you'll be there to protect him, won't you? You'll take care of him..."

I said yes, of course, and she pulled back the curtain and we went out of the little room. Vezzosi was nowhere to be seen. I called out his name and shouted that I was going to open the accordion door, and there he was, immense, bare-chested, sprawled on a sort of dentist's chair much bigger than mine, half-covered by a sheet, like a veiled Christ, and out of shape, wasted, ruined, yet maybe also attractive, glamorous, the perfect image of the last alpha male, truly, and the last possible, ready to be sold and resold thousands and thousands of times over when he was dead. I should have taken a picture of him in that moment, as he kept his eyes closed and gritted his teeth and the tattoo artist loomed, bent over him to finish writing MY SHADOW IS YOURS on his shoulder blade, which was the only still untattooed part of that torso fit for a longshoreman, full of scripts written in all different fonts, small and large, and some were even entire phrases, not just single words. Reading them enchanted me; I repeated them under my breath:

"Never fear. This is your eternal life. Caesar. Ariadne. Mom. Rage, rage against the dying of the light. Fede. Marta. Ivo. Flora. Blind eyes blaze like meteors. Whosoever unceasingly strives upward him we can save. For always. Never against you. Our town. Babbo. Sehnsucht. Harlan. Killer Joe. King Pleasure. Dune. Milena. Epictetus."

He heard me murmuring and opened his eyes.

"Oh, finally! Yes, now you're one handsome dude, Zapata! Let me see your tattoo … Nice, damn … minimalist, just the way I like them … crude and elegant, beautiful, really …"

Then he closed his eyes again and asked me if I knew that I would never stop tattooing myself. That it would become like a drug.

"You think so?"

The tattoo artist halted, turned to look at me, and nodded. Then he went on tattooing.

"This kid is cool, Vittorio. Where did you find him?"

"In the parish church."

"But wasn't he a Communist?"

"Catho-Communist," Vezzosi said, and everybody laughed.

Onward! Onward!

• • •

WE WENT BACK out to walk along the porticoes and he started asking me how long I could go on not telling him about all the hype and hoo-ha that was rising up around him, and that people were going on television to say they were expecting a ray of light and hope from him.

He was advancing in front of me with long strides, and every now and again greeted those who stopped to look at him as he passed by, straight as a spindle and with so much momentum that it must have made everyone believe the idea of stopping him was impossible, because no one even tried to.

"*Ciao! Ciao!*" the smiling Vezzosi called out to those perfect strangers, but also "*Ehi! Ehila!: How's it goin'? How are ya?*" and the perfect strangers seemed like they weren't so much impressed by his newfound popularity as they were sincerely glad to see him.

From the way they smiled when he greeted them, it seemed that they had suddenly run into an old friend in a hurry, and since many of them were up there in years the work of the Archangel's war machine couldn't have had much influence on the affection that I felt radiating from those people. They were his readers, both men and women, and they wished him well.

I shrugged. I had no idea where we were either, and since we didn't know where we had left the Jeep, not even Google could help us all that much, but after a while, Vezzosi remembered having seen a wall with THE CLASH written on it, and from there he somehow managed to reorient himself, and two minutes later we were at the Jeep, which we found decorated with a lovely parking ticket that, for lack of other places to put it, the traffic cop had left on the driver's seat, in clear sight. Vezzosi put on his glasses and studied it carefully.

"Here it says we entered a no-traffic zone without permission and that we parked in a space reserved for residents, and okay, we knew that…" But then, "No, Zapata, this is crazy…It says you can't drive without a windshield, without doors, and without seat belts…"

He scrunched it up and threw it away.

"How can that be possible? If I don't hurt or damage someone else, I can do whatever I want, can't I? What the fuck do they want from me? If I want to drive my car without a windshield, then that's what I do, goddam it! Where are we, in a dictatorship? What the hell happened to personal freedom?"

He rummaged in his jacket pockets.

"We've got to reaffirm it, Zapata. Let's do some drugs!"

"What, right here, out in the open? Everyone will see us…"

"So what?"

We got in the Jeep, and pulled out the Kodak plastic tube and the Diners Club card. He gestured that I should hold out the CD jewel case, and started pouring the cocaine and cutting it into lines. He got six lines out of it, short and not very wide, but still, there were six of them. He leaned forward and was about to snort them, when he turned suddenly to his left.

Right next to him, no more than an arm's length away, was an old woman with blue hair, a purse, and a spotted mutt on a leash. The dog was pissing on the Jeep's tire, and the woman was watching him.

"Would you like some?" Vezzosi asked her, holding out the jewel case with the lines on it, and she, maybe because she hadn't taken her eyes off the dog and the tire, hadn't noticed us, and on seeing that giant of a man with long salt-and-pepper hair, dark eyes, and a faded jeans jacket offering her some white powder, she started, and took a few steps backwards, as the mutt sensed her fear and started barking at us.

"It's really good, has a touch of wild radicchio…"

The old woman opened her mouth to say something, but nothing came out, then she quickly turned and started running away on her short legs, her head down, pulling her dog behind her, that kept on barking, furiously, his neck bent.

Vezzosi watched her running away. He smiled.

"Ah, it's such a long time since I've pulled a stunt like that…"

Then he snorted his three lines, just like that, in the middle of the street, while the whole nation looked on.

"Boy, do I like cocaine! Tell me, Zapata, how many years are there between me and that old woman? Ten? Fifteen? Am I going to end up like that, too? Walking around the city at four in the afternoon trying to get my dog to piss?"

Two little boys were looking at us with their mouths open.

"I don't know, Vezzosi, but at this point I'd say it's time to go."

"Right!"

He handed me the jewel case, started the engine, and we took off with a rumble and a big venomous blast of exhaust, heading straight for the Tower of the Asinelli, which, viewed from far away, looked really tall and a little leaning, but I was surely mistaken. Between a thousand jolts and bounces, I managed to snort my first line and right away I felt it hit me with force, stronger than the others, and when I looked up, I saw the passing image of a traffic cop, who started blowing his whistle furiously. Vezzosi looked at him in the rearview mirror and kept going.

"What does he want, that cop? Damn them. They want to enchain free men, but we won't let them do that, will we, Zapata?"

I turned around, and the cop was standing in the middle of the street, and he was taking our picture with his phone, while Vezzosi was trying to weave his way past enraged pedestrians, indignant cyclists, buses, and one-way signs. As soon as we turned a corner, still in the throes of that rocking like a lifeboat on the high seas, I bent over to snort my second line and my heart started racing. I could feel it pounding in my temples. It speeded up my breathing, too, and I noted that by now we were racing blindly through the pedestrians-only zone, our presence surely having already been notified to the patrols of every branch of law enforcement, and I had to hold on tight to the big handle on the dashboard to keep from being thrown out of the Jeep with all those curves and turns and sudden accelerations, as the engine roared and the tires squealed.

I began to sweat, and my throat closed. I shook myself. What was going on? My forehead was drenched. I told myself I had to calm down, right now. I took a deep breath and exhaled slowly, but it didn't work. My heart kept on pounding away.

In a flash, we bolted out onto the boulevards, and Vezzosi stopped the Jeep.

"There's still one line left for an old writer, or am I wrong?"

"No, it slid off on me, down to the floor."

"Fuck!"

"I'm afraid I'm not feeling very well, Vezzosi."

"No problem, don't think about it. You'll get over it."

He took off again and we stopped at a red light.

"I hadn't spotted that cop at all. He popped out in front of me all of sudden, out from under the porticoes... Even scared me a little... But we didn't hit him, did we? You think they're looking for us?"

In the car next to us, a little girl was looking out at us. She was sitting in a car seat for newborns, too small for her. She had blonde bushy hair, and looked like she was studying me. I smiled at her and she smiled back, maybe surprised that the people in other cars were alive like her.

But am I alive? Have I been alive up to now? And if I were about to die? How would that work, dying? Would I feel pain? Because a cardiac arrest is a heart wound, and wounds hurt, hurt like shit.

The little girl waved at me, and I responded with a thumbs-up. She giggled and gave me a thumbs-up, too, and I saw her mother's head turn.

"We've got to get right onto the autostrada. You see any green arrows? Oh, Zapata, how goes it? A little better?"

"Yeah," I answered, but it wasn't true. My heart had jumped up into my throat, by now, and I wasn't breathing well. I was getting worse, no doubt about it. I couldn't sit still and I had no energy. It was about to happen, fuck. I was about to have a heart attack, like my dad.

And then I felt a pain in my ribs, sharp, and I said to myself: *Here we are, this is the time, it's happening now,* and I groaned loudly and Vezzosi was taken aback and went straight at a rotary. He cut right through the middle of it, crossing the whole thing, and luckily in the middle there was only a flower bed, but we were going fast, and we popped up as if a giant had given the Jeep a head slap, and we came just short of the both of us being thrown out of the car and then mangled by the wheels of our own car or some passing truck.

"What the hell was that horrible sound? Jesus, it scared me," Vezzosi said, and kept going for another hundred meters before stopping in front of a mishmash of road signs and arrows. There was one that indicated the highway, and another, in the opposite direction, the hospital.

"You're all washed out, Zapata. What do you want to do?"

"I don't know. But if I'm meant to die, I'll die, Vezzosi."

That's what I said, and then I closed my eyes. My heart was beating like a drum roll, and I was having trouble breathing. It was over. I was going into a cocaine overdose, nothing to do. I clasped my hands over my chest.

"What do you mean, die, you idiot. What the fuck are you saying? If you want, I'll drop you at the emergency room, but I'd say we should get on our way."

I looked at him, and tried my hardest to mask a hopeful smile.

"Get on our way? How, get on our way. How am I supposed to go anywhere in this condition? I can't even breathe…"

"Look, in a few minutes you'll be over it."

"How do you know?"

"Oh, all right, sure you're a rookie but it's not as if you snorted the snow of Tony Montana. That was some light stuff that I have cut especially so I can snort a lot of it without going to the Creator, just because I like the taste… It's like coffee, not much more…"

I glared at him.

"Really?"

"Sure. But everybody is different, and it affects people differently… You tell me what you want to do, Zapata, I don't want any responsibility. I got to go to Milan in any case…"

And right then, as if it were ashamed of being so agitated over a little coke for old folks, my heartbeat started to slow down.

"Sorry, Zapata, but I absolutely have to see someone there. It's something too important for me."

I inhaled. Exhaled. Closed my eyes.

"And you'd leave me here, in the middle of the road?"

"Yeah, I mean, no, not here. I'll drop you off in front of the emergency room, like in *Trainspotting*..."

Suddenly, it seemed I was feeling better. Plus, if I went to the emergency room, forget Milan, and tomorrow morning Allegra was due to arrive at the central station...

"All right, Zapata, what do I do? I can't stay stopped here, by now they're all looking for us. If they catch us, they put both of us in jail, you know, they shove it up our ass, especially you, because you're young... So, let's go, Zapata, decide. What do we do?"

In the distance, an ambulance siren.

"There they are," he said, "they're coming. Tell me, now, come on..."

I smiled. We're always afraid of dying for doing something wrong, and we're careful about everything, and we watch out for ourselves, and then, instead, all of a sudden, we die, for something stupid, and that's the end of it. And we've left every fucking thing unsaid.

"Oh, so which is it?"

"*Onward! Onward!*"—I started to shout, quoting Gogol, and his dead souls, "*away with the wrinkle that furrows the brow and the stern gloom of the face! At once and suddenly let us plunge into life with all its noiseless clatter and little bells…"*

Vezzosi stared at me for a few seconds.

"That's the spirit, Zapata. Now I'm really beginning to like you!"

And he accelerated toward the highway, which we got to a few minutes later and entered at the top speed that our growling little open wagon could reach, after risking to overturn at least twice as we were going around the long circle of the entrance ramp.

Interstellar

· · ·

OUT OF THE blue came the first notes of "Whole Lotta Love," and it took me a minute to realize it was the ring tone of Vezzosi's phone. He wrinkled his eyebrows, slowed down, struggled to get it out of his jacket pocket, and, when he saw who was calling him, started hitting the screen with his index finger, but the cell slipped out of his hand and fell between the seats, and he cursed Christ and the Madonna.

"Vezzosi!"

He looked at me surprised, and then I heard the silver-toned voice of a girl.

"Daddy, Daddy, are you there? But what is all that wind? Are you at the beach?"

"Hey, hello, honey," he answered, without even trying to get back the phone. "No, I wish, I'm driving…"

He gestured to me to keep quiet.

"Why are you using the speakerphone? I can't hear you very well."

"I'm driving. Wait, I'll pull over…"

He pulled over and stopped in the emergency lane.

"Ah, listen, Daddy, tonight I had an idea…At last, I understood where I want to live."

"Where?"

He stuck his hand down between the seats to pick up the telephone, but he pulled it back with a jerk. He had cut a finger. It was bleeding.

"In Rivendell, Daddy. Do you remember it? It's that little citadel in the mountains where the elves live in *The Lord of the Rings*. It's practically a sort of gorge, completely hidden, you go down a narrow trail and you can't see it until you've almost arrived. It's perched on a cliff among the forests…There are oaks, live oaks, cypress, and all around there are little streams of crystalline water flowing down into the valley…"

"Yes, sure I remember it…It's a marvelous place…"

An enormous truck went right by us and made us pitch to the side and we lost her for a second.

"…those houses of stone and wood, all open to the winds from every direction because there are no panes in the windows, with the arches and the columns and the bay windows and the terraces and the ivy-covered domes and the statues of the lost gods and the warriors, and the dried leaves on the floor that nobody would dream of sweeping away because the leaves aren't dirt, naturally…And then the books, books everywhere, like at your house…"

"Our house..."

"Yes, our house, it's just like ours...Books on the shelves, inside the closets, in the drawers, even on the floor, books and books and books and books, towers of books, but in Rivendell there's time to read them in blessed peace, because really nothing happens there, and it's all in decay, but it's a beautiful decay, Daddy! It's the decay of decays, and it goes back to the dawn of time and it's unstoppable and eternal, and the elves live in it and don't care about repairing anything because for the elves repairing makes no sense and rebuilding even less, *their time on Earth is over*, and so they make do and live out the last days of that bygone beauty with dignity and class, because they've got a ton of class, the elves, no doubt about it, and they know how important it is to end well if you're the last heirs to a glorious past and the present is intolerable and the future doesn't exist anymore...Why are you laughing?"

It wasn't that Vezzosi was laughing. At most, he was grinning, and shaking his head like when you really like what you're hearing, but at the same time it cuts you to the quick.

"No, nothing, nothing."

"No, tell me! Why are you laughing? Look, I'm not talking about you, Daddy...Did you think I was talking about you? Hahahahahahah..."

We laughed, all three of us. I made him a sign that, if he wanted, I could give it a try, to get the telephone, but he shook his head.

"Ah, what a lovely gift of a phone call, my darling girl… You're lighting up my day! I was talking about it just today, *The Lord of the Rings*…"

"Well, that's about it, I would like to live there, among those elegant ruins. And be an elf, too."

"But you're already an elf."

Another truck whizzed by us.

"Yeah, that's true. Always have been, in my heart. But where are you, on the highway? I'm hearing some incredible noises; you want me to call you back?"

"No, no, let's talk now… I'm really glad you called me…"

"Oh, Daddy, there's something else really important that I have to tell you. Fuck, I am so out of it these days, with everything I've got to study…"

"You know I don't like it when you use profanity."

"I'm sorry, but it's incredible that I was about to forget it, it's the reason I called you…"

"Well then, tell me… What's this really important thing?"

"Daddy, there's a movie you just have to see, but it would be ideal if you saw it at the movie theater…"

"You know that's not possible…"

"Yeah, I know, plus it's impossible anyway, because it's a movie from 2014, but you absolutely have to see it. It's called *Interstellar*. I mean, you have to see it immediately, like right now…"

"Is it the one where someone falls through a black hole?"

"Yes."

"Then…"

"Then, what?"

"You know…"

"What?"

"That it's impossible."

"And since when do people watch movies to see things that are possible, Daddy? Listen to me, and watch it ASAP."

"…"

"Daddy…"

"All right, okay, I'll watch it."

"No, seriously… It's an incredible movie, and it's a shame not to see it on the big screen, because it is really immense…"

"You know that there are problems with movie theaters…"

"But, Daddy, you've got to get over this thing… Go to the early show when there's nobody there, sit as far to the front as possible and don't look behind you, no matter what noises you hear… Pretend you're Orpheus."

"Orpheus turned to look…"

"Do what Orpheus should have done, good grief… But, Daddy, don't expect it to be a perfect experience, okay? There is no such thing as a perfect experience, in real life there is always someone there to break your balls…"

"I told you I don't like for you to use profanity."

"Yeah, but if there's somebody there who crunches up a paper bag, or eats potato chips with his mouth open, or says something a little too loud, or starts talking on the telephone, you have to let it slide, okay? You have to make the effort. You have to be above all that."

"But they bother me! They ruin the movie for me!"

"Ignore them. Concentrate on the movie, and forget about them. Don't sit there the whole time thinking about them, and above all, don't go threatening them and slapping them around, because one of these times you're going to get arrested…"

"So I've got to see this movie?"

"Yes, Daddy. It means a lot to me."

"All right, then I'll see it."

"Don't tell me 'I'll see it.' Watch it tonight."

"No, tonight, I can't. We'll watch it together when you come home."

"Daddy, I have to study. For now, I'm not coming home. Plus, it's not a movie that you and I can watch together."

"Why not?"

"Because, no. You'll understand that right away, in the first couple of scenes."

"What am I supposed to understand?"

"If I tell you, it'll ruin everything."

"Tell me why we can't watch it together."

"Because, in the end it's not a science fiction movie, *Interstellar*, I mean, the science fiction is just an excuse, a way to exploit the theory of relativity and all of its space-time distortions for the movies."

"And so, what is it?"

"It's a great movie about love between a father and his daughter, Daddy."

"Really?"

"Yeah, really."

"Then I really do have to see it."

"Yes, and make sure you take some silk hankies with you."

"Why, does it make you cry?"

"Like a fountain."

"Really?"

"Yes."

"Then I'm going. I need a good cry."

"Great. Well, good-bye, Daddy. That's what I wanted to tell you…"

"Good-bye, sweetheart."

"And have a good trip…Where are you going?"

"I'll tell you afterwards."

"Are you with somebody?"

"Yes."

"With that woman?"

"No, I'm not with any woman. I'm with Zapata."

"That arrogant kid? The ball breaker?"

I looked at him with my mouth agape.

"No, no, what are you talking about?"

"If I see him, I'll give him a slap in the face."

"Come on, drop it, forget about it."

"I know we're on speakerphone and he can hear me too…I'm saying it on purpose. When I come back to Italy,

I'm coming to get you, little boy. Nobody touches my father, understand?"

"Come on, drop it. Let's change the subject, please…"

"Yeah, let's. You, Daddy, how are you doing, really?"

"I'm fine. And you?"

"Great. Like a queen. Thanks to you. But are you really okay? Are you sure?"

"Sure, why are you asking…"

"Well, the email that you sent me last night…"

"Ah… but there's really nothing, think nothing of it."

"Hard not to think about it, you know? To tell you the truth, I was a little hurt. I know how you are, but it seemed strange to me, sad… Not nice, you know? Not like you. It worried me a little…"

"No, please, it's just nighttime thoughts… Forget it, I shouldn't have sent it to you. Don't worry, there's no need to."

"What the fuck does that mean, Daddy, don't worry about it? You sent me a list of writer suicides…"

He looked at me, shook his head.

"No, that can't be right."

"But it is, actually."

"But how, I deleted them… and anyway, there's nothing strange about it, it was a literary thing…"

"Ah, come off it, Daddy."

"I'm sorry, honey."

"All those desperate men and women who offed themselves… It upset me."

"I'm really sorry."

"But you'd tell me if there was really something wrong, wouldn't you?"

"Certainly."

"Yeah, my ass you would."

"I promise you, I would tell you, if there were something wrong, and anyway, everything is fine, believe me, please..."

"Are you driving the Jeep?"

"Yes."

"Did you open it up?"

"Yes."

"And did you take the windshield down?"

"Yes."

"And you're on the highway..."

"Yes."

"You've been to Bologna, to Stefano's, to get yourself that shadow tattoo you wrote me about, right?"

"Busybody!"

"Ahahahah, I always get you, Daddy. So that means there really is something wrong..."

"Good-bye, now, honey. Don't worry. Everything's fine."

"Bye, Daddy. Be careful, now, especially about that woman."

"Ciao."

"I mean it."

"Ciao." And he hung up."

We got back on the road, and he started cursing like I'd never heard anyone curse before. He kept on shouting that he'd deleted it, *the list of the shithead writer suicides*, he was sure he had deleted it, and then more horrible curses for ten minutes or more, his fist banging on the steering wheel, until he started gasping for air, and he calmed down and stared straight ahead, scowling.

After twenty kilometers or so at fifty an hour, I wondered if it was possible to see the movie right away. I pulled my PC out of my pack and found the link. We stopped at a service area to fill up and traded places, and there I was behind that unpadded wheel and that elongated metallic dashboard, crammed with levers and quadrants all around a big round tachometer that indicated our speed in miles per hour. I gave it a shot of gas and heard the motor get agitated before going back to gurgling like a sleeping dragon.

"You think I'll be able to drive this thing, Vezzosi?"

"Sure, it's easy as pie. How do I put these things on?"

I showed him how to use the earplugs, clicked to start up *Interstellar*, and put it in first, but I screwed up on the clutch and the car stopped and the engine shut off.

Vezzosi smiled.

"That always used to happen to me, with my buddy's Ferrari…"

"What?"

"Come on, Zapata, get with it. More delicate with the clutch and heavier on the gas… This donkey wants to look a man in the face, show her who you are."

I restarted the engine, shoved the stick into first, gave it a little more gas, and, with lurches and jolts, we got on our way, and after less than ten minutes of the movie, Vezzosi started crying—I mean, he was sobbing—and he went on like that practically nonstop until the end, when, even though we were traveling at a snail's pace, being passed by everyone, even by hat-sporting old codgers, even by trailers, we were at the gates of Milan.

In the meantime, I had recovered completely. Driving was good for me. I was always a little agitated, I gritted my teeth and my brain was spinning like a top, my thoughts twisting around each other, and practically I had done nothing else but smile for two hours in a row across the plain of the Po River valley that stretched endlessly beside me, but I had recovered.

I wasn't fainting anymore.

I wasn't dying anymore.

Presidential Suite

. . .

WHEN WE GOT into the center of Milan, it was already eight o'clock and we went directly to this luxury hotel where Vezzosi had reserved two rooms. His, the manager explained to us, was the presidential suite. It had a fifty-square-meter living room with a view of the downtown, a double bedroom, three LED-screen TVs, two minibars, and two baths.

Vezzosi was astonished and seemed to feel ashamed of all that pomp, and asked if there was also another one just like it for the young *Professor De Vito*, but they informed him that when it came to presidential suites, there was only one, and I started laughing and said that all I needed was a bed of leaves, and he called me an imbecile under his breath.

We went up in the elevator with the manager and another henchman, and when I got out at the first stop, Vezzosi said he'd be expecting me in an hour.

"For our cocktail in bathrobes…"

The manager chimed in, asking if he could send up a bottle of Dom Perignon, and Vezzosi thanked him regally and winked at me, delighted by the misinterpretation, while the elevator doors were closing and they disappeared, toward the top floor and the presidential suite.

My room was beautiful—for sure I had never ever been, and in any case will never be again, in such a luxurious place—and even though I suddenly felt exhausted, instead of throwing myself on the bed, I went into the bathroom, got naked, took the plastic wrap off my chest, admired Allegra's tattoo, and, after resolving the problems posed by all the levers and buttons and faucets of that super bathtub, enjoyed the first hydro-massage of my life, and I enjoyed it so much that I fell asleep in there, in that gurgling whirlpool of bubbles, and when I woke up, for a second I couldn't remember anymore where I was and what I was doing, like what happens to characters in books or movies, and that, too, was a first, and was really to my liking.

The world, in the meantime, had gone crazy. My profile had reached almost a hundred thousand followers, and our picture was on the home pages of all the Italian newspapers and all the news sites, and next to the pic of the Jeep that he had immediately popped and posted was the smiling headshot of the cop in Bologna, who had declared: *I'm really sorry that Maestro Vezzosi didn't pull over. I would never have given him a ticket! I just wanted to shake his hand and help him get out of the pedestrian zone, which he had certainly entered by mistake, I would have been very, very happy to escort him!!! I adore his novel!!!*

I called the Archangel.

"Are we satisfied, Zapata?"

"Huh, yeah, sure, in two days I've garnered almost a hundred thousand followers...Can you explain to me how that's possible?"

"That seems like a lot to you? I thought we could do better than that, to tell you the truth...but they're all happy, so that's fine with me..."

"So what do I have to do, then? You want more pictures? A video? Because today has been rather complicated..."

"No, no problem. Don't do anything, tomorrow it'll all be over. We've already pulled the plug."

"Pulled the plug?"

"Yeah, it's over. Things last for a day, two at the most, then it's on to something else..."

"What do you mean?...What about all those people?"

"Look, Zapata, maybe you haven't gotten it yet, but people are imbeciles...They don't have shit to do from morning to night, and so they're all there with their telephones in hand or at their computers...and they react right away, understand? While they're shooting the shit or fighting with other imbeciles like themselves, or reviewing restaurants and hotels they've never been to, or buying three-euro T-shirts and cute little dresses they wear once and throw away, they also give you a like...What's it cost them? But it's not worth shit, Zapata, how can I put it to you...The next day, they've all forgotten it, that's the way it works...But now I've got to let you go, I'm playing tennis..."

"Oh, sorry, I thought you were on your computer."

"The computer? I'm on it as little as possible, the computer. It's my Archangelini who takes care of keeping the ship on course..."

"And who are they?"

"Kids from junior high, at most high-schoolers...Child labor, sure, but they have a good time, and anyway, we're talking that level of brain power...no, even lower..."

"And so, you're not always online."

"Me? You think Escobar took drugs? Or did he make money getting other people to take it, the cocaine? Because, it's like a drug, you know? It works exactly like a drug...But I wanted to tell you that I started reading it, the book, your friend's book, shit...I don't know much about literature, but it is really cool...I mean, I don't know how to put it, it makes you want to live inside it, to be able to be there with him and do the things he does...You're one lucky guy, Zapata, very lucky. If I come to the fair, will you introduce me? I'll bring Carlita, too. Both of us would really like to shake his hand...So, what do you say?"

I slipped into my terrycloth robe, went up to the top floor, and knocked on Vezzosi's door. I heard him shout *Onward, Savoy!* and I went in. He was sitting at a big glass table in front of the spectacle of the thousands of lights shining in the Milanese night, and on the table was a silver tray with a dozen lines of coke, thin as blades of grass, all the same length.

"Let's get this straight, Zapata," he declared, "this fucking luxury is not for me. It's for jerks, but there are times when it's consoling, no denying it, and right now I need solace and comfort, after that journey through hell we were on...And, to give you the whole story, I got this suite to impress Milena, but I don't know anymore if all this fucking opulence is something she'll like or not...Maybe not, who knows, let's hope it is...But, on the other hand, I also didn't want to get depressed or depress her by offering her hospitality in some banal place, or in a more modest hotel...I figured the best was better than the worst, no? Was I wrong? All things considered, I don't know, Zapata, I don't know...I'm confused, very confused..."

He sat there looking out at the view through the glass wall.

"Ah, so I had better leave right away, then."

He turned to look at me, lost in thought.

"Why?"

"I don't know, I imagine you'll want some intimacy with this woman..."

"No, what's got into your head? Milena is coming later, to the restaurant, not here. You think I'd want her to see me like this?"

And he pointed at all those lines that I couldn't stop staring at. There were so many, one next to the other, identical, perfectly precise.

"These are for us," he said, and he bent over to snort one of them.

When he invited me to take my turn, I realized how much I'd been hoping that he would. What the fuck was happening to me, I had no idea, but I snorted two, one after the other, and there it was again, that bitter sensation, the suddenly dry nose, the lighting of the fire inside, the euphoria of a child, and immediately the necessity, or rather the need, to keep everything hidden, to keep everything under control. Invisible. Private. Mine and only mine. Burning inside and impassive on the outside. And as my heart proudly started to accelerate, it no longer counted in the least that just a few hours earlier I had been convinced I was going to die from that stuff. I liked it, and so much for that.

"You like this drug, eh, Zapata?"

I flinched. Was it so obvious?

"I saw it coming. You can't take your eyes off it. That's the way it is at the beginning…"

He leaned over to snort another line.

"Anyway, the secret is to make the lines thin, to trick your brain, because it's important to know that there's a part of your brain that thinks and another part that perceives, and they're different, and I discovered a way to trick both of them. No, you *have to* trick both of them, otherwise you can't live…So, you think you've really done a lot of it, but in reality you've only done a little…Come on, have another…"

Each of us snorted another line, and we leaned against the backs of those elegant chairs, looking out at Milan shining brightly beyond the glass.

"Who is this Milena, Vezzosi?"

"Milena Zucchi is the woman of my life. The reason why we're here. The only reason."

"And the speech at the fair?"

"An excuse."

"An excuse?"

"Yeah, sure, an excuse. Bullshit."

"What do you mean?"

"If tonight it doesn't go well with Milena, there won't be any speech, Zapata. We'll get back in the Jeep and drive back home during the night."

"And all those people?"

"What people?"

He stared at me and I had to look away.

"I don't know... There'll be a lot of people who come to hear you, no?"

"I don't give a shit about the people. Zero. All I care about is Milena."

"But who is she, am I allowed to know?"

"Milena is the heroine of the book... the one you haven't read, you little dickhead..."

"But thanks a million for the dedication, my mother was moved to tears... Shall we call her?"

"Sure."

I digited the number and passed him the phone.

"My dear Franca!" he chimed, with a high-pitched voice that I had never heard from him before. "This is Vittorio Vezzosi, your son's driver."

They went on talking for quite a while. He listened, mostly. Every now and again he said *thank you*, or *Sure*, and nodded.

He told Mama a bunch of nice things, like I was a *little race-horse*, that I had *a great character*, and that one day I was going to do *something big*. They said good-bye and he gave me back the phone. I held it up to my ear and there was Mama, who was still thanking him with a broken voice, then she hung up.

"She's nice, Franca. She told me about your father. I'm, sorry, I didn't know it had happened so recently…He deserves a toast…Where did they leave that little decanter?"

He got up, went into the bedroom, and came back with the bottle of Dom Perignon, dripping along the way, and we drank a toast to our dads, who must have been very different people, however. His, he told me, was called The Beast.

"Tell me about this Milena."

"No, that's not possible."

"Why not?"

"Because no. You can't recount your youth."

"No?"

"For sure, no…How is it possible to recount the passion, the rage, the fear, the deathly boredom, the hopes and the frustrations and the marvelous and total void of those days without memory that never end. And the pain, all the pain, and the immense joy, exhilarating and stupid as shit, and yet burning and blessed…No, there's no way…Only the greatest can do it…And then there's also the fact of having lived it in that particular moment, and in those years which were the best ever, in the whole history of the world. Those years that really cannot be recounted, and that could only have been lived and experienced. You had to be there. When were you born? 2000?"

"'97."

"Okay, figure that Milena and I got together twenty years before you were born. No, nineteen. In '78. When Argentina won the World Cup on that field full of confetti... There were still hippies, people were shooting up in the piazzas, and I was fourteen years old and did nothing else but read science fiction and listen to music in my room, and then one day Neil Young came to do a concert in Viareggio with Crazy Horse, and Fede and I went to see him on our Vespa 50s... Try to imagine parking a Vespa next to the Pini Stadium, going in to see Neil Young, who plays the songs you've been listening to all winter... And then Milena arrives... The first day I saw her, she was standing outside of my school, laughing... wearing a sheepskin coat and an Invicta backpack, and it was enough to make you faint, shit... She was gorgeous..."

He got up and went over to the glass. For a long time, he was silent. Who knows what he was really looking at out there? The only thing you could see were the bright lights and the black night.

"We got together and stayed together for a few years, and then one night she dropped me. It was the end of summer and there was a Gloria Gaynor concert and an absurd sunset, fuck, bleeding... I've never again seen a sunset like that, the only thing missing was the descent of the Valkyries down from the clouds to take me away... And maybe that would have been better, because then everything fell apart."

He drank the last bit of champagne from his glass.

"I've never forgotten Milena, and in all those years that came afterwards I practically did nothing else but try to survive... That's the story..."

And he fell silent.

A full minute of silence went by.

"Sorry, Vittorio, hold on a second, because I need to get this straight... That is, you're telling me that, actually, all of us are here in Milan so that you can see a woman again who you were with in high school, a thousand years ago?"

He turned toward me very slowly.

"Yeah, why?"

He smiled.

"Come on..."

"Come on, what?"

"That's not true..."

"Why not?"

"No, it's that... Come on, it's not true, there must be something else... That can't be true."

He stared at me, enormous.

"You think it's bullshit?"

"No, it's that something like that is unreal. It can't be real."

He sat down again at the table, poured himself some more champagne.

"But, instead, it is real."

"But, Vezzosi, with all due respect, this is something that's seriously crazy. I mean, really, I'm sorry... Something out of Looney Tunes. For people who need to be locked up.... How many years have gone by? Computers probably still didn't exist when you two…"

"There were already fucking computers breaking our balls…"

"Yeah, okay, there were already computers, but, seriously, come on…It sounds like something out of a nineteenth-century romantic novel, it can't be true…"

"But why not?"

"What do you mean, why not? Because, after all this time, it's not possible that you're still in love with that girl, who, by the way, is no longer a girl…And you're not a kid yourself…"

He pursed his lips.

"Well, listen to what a brilliant intuition has come out of the mouth of our Zapata…And why not? Why can't I still be in love with her, huh?"

"Because no, I'm sorry, it's out of the question. You've lived in the meantime, and so has she…She probably has kids…"

"No, she doesn't have kids."

"All right, she doesn't have kids, but let's face it, everything in the world has changed in the years that have passed, and along with the world, your life has changed, no? You're not the same person who went to concerts on your Vespa, isn't that right? There, and so it's not possible that you're still there thinking about her, with everything that's happened to you since then…Because a few things have happened to you, no? Nice things, too, even very nice…"

He looked at me and smiled, as though he had every right in the world to see it the way he did and he was just waiting for me to realize it, too.

"Come on, Vittorio, come off it. I don't believe it. It's not true…"

"Tell me why it's not true. Explain it to me exactly."

"Why, why, why. Because at some point, the present takes the place of the past, and things are forgotten, no? All things, the nice things and the ugly things… And that's true of people, too… Everyone forgets everything and everybody. Me too. The past falls into oblivion, the cancellation of all memories… I've forgotten about my father, for example…"

"That's not true."

"But it is true. I don't think of him anymore."

"It's not true, you imbecile. You'll come to realize it."

"It's my business, damn it!"

"You'll see."

"…"

"…"

"And anyway, I think that, all things considered, it's only right, you understand that, Vezzosi? More than that, it's *natural* to forget about things and people, because otherwise we couldn't move on with our lives… What kind of life would that be, someone who chases a memory for thirty years? We can't just let the past stay there and haunt us and torment us forever. At some point, it has to go away, no?"

He looked at me for a long time, then a smile came over his face, a bitter smile.

"You know, Zapata, I don't know what it means to *move on*, and I'll tell you, the idea has always made me mad as hell, this thing about moving on...How can you move on when everything that you love and want, everything you live for, and even what you are, damn it, has been left behind, huh? On to where, where was I supposed to move on to? Toward what, if ahead of me there was nothing? No, Zapata, I've never been able to move on..."

The smile vanished, and he turned serious.

"My past has never passed, Zapata. It's still here, right next to me. I can see it, even now."

He thrust one arm forward and clenched his fist in the air.

"I can touch it."

He got up and went back to the window.

"Now, get out of here, Zapata, before you start laughing at me. I've already put on enough of a show."

"No, what are you saying... Tell me more..."

He took a deep breath, and let it out slowly.

"What more do you want to know?"

"After you broke up, what happened? Did you try to win her back?"

"Yeah, sure I tried. For years, I tried, like an idiot... But it was useless. It was as though our roads divided that day."

"And so, how long has it been since you last saw her?"

"Quite a while."

"How long?"

"Thirty-five years."

"How many?"

He turned around, and he was smiling.

"What's this, Zapata? Are you playing the role of the stupid movie character who pretends not to believe his own ears and keeps repeating the same lines?"

"No, sorry..."

"I know that I'm crazy, I know...But you have to understand that I am in love with her and I will always be in love with her, Zapata...And it's not a question of beauty, even if, actually, Milena is very beautiful, as you'll see...It's that I love her and I always will, and I couldn't give a shit that she's fifty-four years old and she's got wrinkles, because even so I'll love her wrinkles, too, understand? No, I'll love her wrinkles more than anything else...Fuck, I'd love her even if she were scarred and hunchbacked and lame..."

"Fifty-four? Milena is *fifty-four years old*?"

"Yeah, we're almost the same age. I'm two months older."

We looked at each other for a few seconds without saying anything.

"You must have at least talked to each other by phone in all these years."

"No, I never called her.

"And why not?"

"Uhhh...I don't know. Maybe I was afraid she wouldn't answer, or that she'd answer just out of courtesy...We've exchanged messages, though. I mean, I send her messages on Christmas, New Year's Eve, Easter, on her birthday... Sometimes she answers, sometimes no. But, look, in this whole story there is something important that I haven't told you, Zapata.

"And what's that?"

"She thinks about me, I'm sure of it. I know it and I've always known it."

He raised his forefinger to shut me up and went back to sit at the table.

"Hold on, Zapata, because it's important that you at least understand this... Look, Joan Didion says it better than anybody, this thing, I think in *Democracy*... In that book, there are two characters who have always loved each other, but they've never managed to get together, okay? Mistaken marriages, life's misadventures, drugs, deaths, revolutions, nuclear tests in the Pacific, all the classic things that nobody narrates better than old Joan... But, in the end, when they find each other, she says this to him... I know it by heart, listen... *Anyway, we've been together. We've been together all our lives. If you also count all the time we've spent thinking of each other.*"

And then he shut up and stared at me, and seconds went by, and I could stay silent, too, sure. Not respond. Let it go. Anyway, what difference did it make? But no.

"Yeah, but this is an abyss, Vezzosi. No, it's *the abyss*. You can fall down into it and never come out again... You can lose your mind, over this thing, because, excuse me, but if you don't even talk with a woman, how can you tell that she thinks about you? Come on, with all due respect, only people who are delusional talk this way..."

He was shaking his head.

"Stalkers, madmen... People who are always convinced they know what others are thinking..."

"No, you don't understand. Milena thinks about me and she always has. There's no doubt about it. I know it."

"Vezzosi, excuse me, but now I have to tell you this... Don't get mad, okay? But listen to me... If she dumped you thirty-five years ago and after that you've never even talked to each other by phone, and she doesn't even respond to your messages..."

"Yeah?"

"No, look... Hasn't it ever crossed your mind that this middle-aged lady is trying to tell you something that you don't want to understand?"

Bitter smile.

"You know, I get you, Zapata... Normal people reason the way you do... I was wrong to tell you the story, I should have kept the secret, it's all the same anyway... And I'll tell you something else, it was a mistake to bring you here with me, I should have left you in Florence to keep an eye on the house..."

"What are you saying..."

"No, I mean it... You know why I brought you here?"

"No, why?"

"Because when you started screaming at the top of your voice that you were madly in love with this Alice, who didn't want you, I believed you, understand?

What? I swallowed.

"Sorry? And when would that have been?"

"So, you don't remember, eh? At Mamadou's farewell party, at the disco... Fuck, were you bombed... You were walking around bare-chested and barefoot, telling everybody that your father was dead, and that you had forgotten him and that you couldn't forgive yourself, and that you were madly... *madly*, you screamed... in love with a woman but that you had just betrayed her and so you were on your way to hell, and you deserved it, to go to hell... But you were laughing, understand? As if you were not afraid, neither of hell nor of anything... And I thought: here he is, finally I've found the one who suffers for everyone, and drinks for everyone, and dreams for everyone... Here he is, the poet... But I was wrong: you don't understand a fucking thing and you're also a bourgeois and you've got no faith in anything and you don't know shit about life or about women, and you know why?"

"No, you tell me..."

"Because on one of these disastrous nights of my shitty life I was lying out on the terrace, reading the *Volcano*, okay? And I was drinking frozen gin and tonics one after another from six-thirty on and I had snorted a fair amount of our little sister here and I was waiting for two lap dancers to give me and Mamadou blow jobs, and so, according to the conventional wisdom, I was impersonating the figure of the happiest man in the world, okay? So, at that moment, the telephone rings and it's her, with her voice that hasn't changed one bit, who says to me, *Ciao, Victor, this is Milena*. Victor, she calls me, and no one has ever called me Victor, only her. RCA Victor, we used to joke, when she and I spent entire afternoons in my room, listening to Billy Joel... My heart leaps to my throat, Zapata, really, and I jump to my feet and fall to the ground, book, drug, gin and tonic, tray, and table, and Mamadou rushes over to me because he thinks I've had a heart attack, like that time at the 'Costume Football' match, and meanwhile Milena tells me she's in Milan working with her husband, who is someone who handles public relations and organizes conferences, and she tells me that there's this 1980s Fair that they're organizing together, and that for the inauguration they've invited the quiz show host Gerry Scotti, but that Gerry, God bless his little heart, had a problem at the last minute and so she had thought about asking me, *given that you're considered a kind of symbol of those years by way of the great success of your book*, that's how she put it, if I felt like presiding at the inauguration. She knew that I was *a little reluctant to travel and speak in public*, but she was in a fix and was asking me for help."

"And you?"

"I couldn't even talk... Oh, Zapata, the words just wouldn't come, really... In an instant I was overcome with a raging headache and my heart was pounding in my temples, and so I went back to sit down, and in those seconds that went by, maybe she thought that I was about to say no, and she asked me another time, to go to Milan to present the 1980s Fair, and added a *Please* and I heard her voice breaking as she whispered: *I'm asking you in the name of everything that there was between us, Victor…"*

He poured himself some more champagne and gulped it down.

"Okay, Vezzosi, I got it, but excuse me…"

"No!" he shouted, pointing his finger at me. "No. Shut up! Just shut up! I know what you're going to say: that now she needs me and can say anything, but that's not what she really thinks, I know that…Plus, women aren't like us, they never forget those they've loved…Believe me, Zapata, Joan Didion was right and I'm right, too, and Milena has never forgotten me…"

"All right, okay…Let's assume that's the way it is…And then? What happened?"

"It happened that I accepted, naturally…And as soon as I'd accepted, I felt happier than I'd felt in a lifetime, and she thanked me profusely, and she started laughing when I said that, if she had asked me, I would have agreed to present a show of Carpathian shepherd dogs…"

He snorted a line, and I did one, too. His eyes were shiny.

"Then we started to call each other, pretty often, too, with the excuse of organizing the event…That's what she calls it, the *event*…Apparently, it's a big deal, this fair. People come to it from abroad, because, get this, Zapata, it seems that Italy is the worldwide center of nostalgia, the country that suffers the most from remembering how things were before…"

He gave me the umbrella salute, his right hand slapping the inside of his left elbow.

"And then one night I tried going a little deeper, and she let it all out and told me there were problems between her and her husband because he had started up with a younger woman and didn't care about her anymore, and they fought a lot, and one time he had even told her that she had become an old witch and he didn't want to see her anymore...But she recounted it without any suffering, understand? It was a closed wound...No pain, Lucio Battisti would have said...And then I started thinking that maybe there was a crack opening up in the shitty destiny that I'd been given...Maybe there was a sort of crawl space I could slip into, and I started hoping like a little kid, and from that moment everything changed for me, totally..."

He threw his arms open, smiled.

"I mean, my life, my poor desperate life, could maybe change and turn itself around, understand, Zapata? Maybe I wasn't destined to stay shut up inside that house until the end of time, remembering the past and worrying about my plants and flowers and buying fish and being the custodian of all those books and movies..."

His eyes were flashing.

"I went into a tizzy...I started counting the days, and the tension kept mounting...In fact, I sleep hardly at all and badly, I forget to eat, I drink like a fish, and I've started hitting it hard with our little sister here..."

"Hold on, when did all this happen?"

"Now..." He smiled. "Now, Zapata, in the last few days...More or less when you came on the scene...Right before I went to London to see my little girl…Ah, what a wonderful vacation…Just think, we spent the last day at Kew Gardens, with the azaleas in bloom and those rarest of palm trees in that Victorian conservatory, and then, after a great dinner in a fantastic restaurant where we talked all night about Superstudio and Twombly and the *O-toro* and Phoebe Philo, I walked her to a taxi because the next morning she had to get up early to study, and I stayed on my own, right in the middle of Mayfair, and instead of feeling my heart break like every time the kid goes away, that time I felt good, at peace, full of energy…It was a lovely cool evening, with that brisk London breeze and the streets were full of boys and girls out to have a good time, and I was overcome with that optimism of that young kid in the 1980s when I went to New York and life was a blank page and I felt like I could do anything and that everything would go well, and so I take out my telephone, open up WhatsApp, see that Milena is online and I call her…Just like that, you know, without thinking…I know I shouldn't, that it's something you don't do, because in Italy it's already after midnight and you never call a woman at night, when you've been drinking and you miss her so much…But by now I've made the call and she answers right away, all happy, and says she's really glad to hear me, and I in the meantime have already gone down the Connaught hill and arrived in Berkeley Square and I've stopped in front of the shop window of an auction house because there was a small painting by Basquiat on display…One of his crowned laughing heads, you know, and it seems like it's laughing at me, too, that it's encouraging me, and so I say it all, Zapata...the truth...that I've always loved her and that for me nothing has ever changed and that I still want her at all costs...I tell her that there are still a lot of beautiful things I can do in life, lots of them, because I practically haven't seen anything of the world and haven't done anything, I'm a misfit...And anyway, I tell her I want to see the flowering of the cherry blossoms in Japan, the whales, eternal Mexico, the aurora borealis, the Pacific Ocean...I tell her I want to go to the equator and feel the sun beating down on the top of my head, and then I want to go to Antarctica, to Brasília to see the buildings by Niemeyer, to Saint Petersburg, Tierra del Fuego, South Africa, New Zealand, Jerusalem, to Vancouver to look for the shack where Malcolm Lowry lived...But I can only do all of these things with her, because without her they're not worth anything, and I'm not worth anything either..."

"And she?"

"She starts crying, Zapata. She cries her eyes out, and doesn't say anything, and so I up the ante and I tell her about the endless tragedy my life has been without her, and I lay it out to her really nice, believe me, really nice, like I've never done before...I go on for an hour there, in Mayfair, in front of Basquiat's king, and I even make her laugh, and in the end, I stick in the phrase by Joan Didion, and she remains silent for a few seconds and she tells me that she, too, has always thought about me all these years, and that she has never forgotten me either. And she hangs up. Understand, Zapata? And now I'm going to see her. We're going to dinner together. She and I."

I jumped up and went over to hug him, that bear, and while we're hugging, he says to me in my ear:

"Oh, you're coming too, I'm serious . . . I got it all booked . . . You'll be at another table, naturally, but you're coming, too, that way if I should need some advice, I give you a sign and we meet in the bathroom, okay?"

I slipped out of the hug and went over to the window to look out, because I didn't want him to notice the tears in my eyes.

"Sure, I'll come, Vezzosi," I said.

And then I turned around and saw him sitting there at that glass table, the lines of coke deployed in front of him like they were protecting him, hair tousled and defenseless, and a total liar, in love with a ghost, in thrall to his last remaining dream, and I sensed that in some way our fates were tied to each other, and if the dinner went badly, I would have to pick him up with a spoon, but if it went well . . . if, for some reason, Vezzosi succeeded in winning back Milena, then I would be able to win back Allegra and I would marry her and we would spend the rest of our lives together. I was on the verge of tears, but I managed to contain myself, and I even smiled and said, with my voice shaking:

"But if we've got this important commitment tonight, let's put this champagne and drugs away, Vezzosi! We've got to keep our heads clear! Come on, let's get a nice shower and dress up! Sprinkle our bodies with drops of fragrance, comb ourselves with hair oil, and throw ourselves off the absurd precipice of the life of romance!"

And he wrinkled his eyebrows.

"Who is it that said that?"

"Me."

He burst out laughing and saw me to the door; then he opened it, put his hand on my shoulder, and looked me in the eye, dead serious.

"What do you think, Zapata, after a shower, should I also do a hopeful bidet, or is that bad luck?"

A Dynamite Chick
of Fifty-Four

. . .

WE WERE SITTING at my table because Vezzosi didn't want Milena to see him waiting for her all alone, *like he was desperate.*

"I've been playing that all my life, the downtrodden writer, damn it, even before I started to write, and it has never done me any good, only defeats and disasters. Tonight, I want to start out in a different way: charged up, gallant, decisive, a winner…"

His gaze went blank, and he started shaking his head.

"But no, no…What am I saying, what the fuck am I saying…Jesus, Mary, and Joseph, Zapata, have I done the right thing putting in motion this whole pantomime? And if she doesn't come?"

"She will, she will, of course she will."

"But why do you say that, what's with this tone of contempt, I don't like it at all…Plus, it's all wrong, as though

Milena had everything to gain by coming here tonight...I'm telling you, that's not how it is..."

"Vittorio, come on... You're a superstar, and she's a woman of a certain age who needs you...Of course she's coming..."

He laughed.

"Me a superstar and she a lady of a certain age? You crack me up, Zapata...A *superstar*...But wasn't I the product of a criminal system? Wasn't I someone who had nothing more than a stroke of luck? Wasn't I Mr. Magoo? You really do crack me up..."

He was laughing so hard I blushed.

"Yes, but apart from those things I said that night, for which I now apologize, Milena is only three years younger than my mother..."

"Don't ever apologize, Zapata. That's when they jump all over you. And Milena is gorgeous, you'll see."

"Okay, maybe she was...Vezzosi, I'm telling you, prepare yourself, because when a lady arrives with short hair and a purse, you're going to take a hit..."

He raised his hands to his face.

"Well, you really don't understand shit. The problem is not her, it's me. What happens if I can't deal with it? I mean, for example, if I faint? Because it could happen, Zapata, I'm not kidding."

"Come on, get over it..."

"No, because I...I mean, you might see me like this now, but I'm the sensitive type, really sensitive, and I'm afraid I'll get too agitated when I see her, I mean get too emotional, and start shaking and stuttering like a jerk, and then maybe faint right in front of her…"

"Oh, what a crock, come on… Calm down, it's nothing…"

"What do you mean, it's nothing. This is a question of life and death, Zapata. How will I seem to her? Will I make a good impression? Because she hasn't seen me either, since I was a strapping young lad, an athlete… But today, with this white hair and this fucking flab that I'm carrying around, damn all that eating and drinking… The only good thing is since I'm fat, I don't have wrinkles on my face… But I can't disappoint her, Zapata, I can't afford that, I've got to still please her at least a little, physically, I mean, if not, it's all over… How does this shirt look on me? You like it?"

He had put on a white cotton shirt, a little too big but rather nice, jeans, and his usual boots with the square toes. He was on the edge between drunk and almost drunk, and so was I.

"Let's have a drink, Zapata."

He poured both of us another glass of Bourgogne, a spectacular taste of bread crust and stewed fruit, and declaimed as he raised his glass toward me:

"To good luck!"

The other tables all turned to look. They had recognized him, naturally. Mama had written to me that they had talked about him on the nightly news. It was all murmurs, glances, tapping on telephones, but thankfully, no one came over to the table.

He had booked in a little restaurant hidden in one of the side streets near the cathedral, not luxurious but elegant and discreet, and considered *the best in the city for fish*, as the taxi driver had declared letting us off behind the Palazzo Reale.

"She's fifteen minutes late, Zapata. That means she's not coming. She's never late. I know her. She hates being late."

"You knew her when she was not much older than a little girl."

"That's true, too...So maybe she'll still come? What do you think?"

"Sure, she'll come."

"Let's hope so. And what do we do while we're waiting? Shall we take a look at the menu? They've got crab imperial, Zapata, look. You like it? Scallops, shrimp, sea urchins, white bream, anchovies San Filippo...all really enticing stuff...When I was in Rome, a thousand years ago, I always went to a fantastic place where all the waiters called me 'Maestro,' and they were so nice to me and made me pasta with dates, which are prohibited."

"Dates, prohibited? But they sell them in supermarkets..."

"Sea dates, Zapata. Boy, you really have no knowledge of the world. You're like an infant..."

"Listen, my dear *Maestro*...before this Milena gets here...the infant has on his telephone twenty messages from Passini, asking him if your lordship is going to speak or not, tomorrow, and about what...What do I tell him?"

"Passini? What the fuck does Passini have to do with it?"

And, in that moment, there came through the door a

woman like few I have ever seen, and all of them in movies or on television, never in real life. Vezzosi stood up and mumbled:

"There she is."

At fifty-four, Milena still succeeded in making half the restaurant turn to look as she came toward us with an imperceptible limp and a slight smile on her delicate ivory-skin face, surely never even grazed by the gaze of a plastic surgeon and ever so slightly streaked by smile lines, adorned with a sprinkling of freckles that, rather than defuse that almost classical beauty, rendered it earthy, even carnal.

She was advancing slowly, a stars and stripes helmet in hand, with a self-assurance so serene that it stopped just a millimeter short of spilling over into self-display, and while the billowy cascade of copper-colored hair appeared to light up as she passed under the restaurant's LED lighting, her faded-to-death but untorn jeans, the Texas boots, the light Saharan jacket over a thick-cotton white shirt, and the silver slave-bracelets dissociated her from the idea that she could be as old as she was, Milena looked like she knew quite well that she was no longer young, and she didn't even wish to seem so.

She was a dynamite chick of fifty-four, free and self-assured, and she dressed as she liked, and as she had always dressed. A live, true, real woman, who had lived without letting herself be crushed by life, and you could tell she still had a fire burning inside, because she shone, damn it, and was going to be my perpetual erotic dream.

When she finally turned her gaze to Vezzosi, her eyes sparkled. Who knows, maybe for her, too, the past wasn't past, and if she stretched a hand out into the air, she could still touch it.

She stopped in front of us, took Vezzosi's face in her hands, and let out a laugh of enjoyment. Then, with the voice of a little girl, she said:

"Victor! Ciao!"

She hugged him, and she held him close a good long time, and when they released, Vezzosi had shiny eyes. He cleared his throat and introduced me:

"Milena, let me introduce you to Professor Emiliano De Vito."

I performed a slight bow. If my feet hadn't been wearing the usual Stan Smiths, I would have clicked my heels.

"Also known as Zapata," he added, and she granted me a smile.

Vezzosi called out to a waiter:

"Corton-Charlemagne de Coche-Dury, for us and for Professor De Vito!"

Then they went to their table, which was not far from mine, and talked intensely the whole evening. They laughed a lot. What they ordered was also served to me. Lobster, crab imperial, sea urchins. All delicious things that I had never had, and the wine was paradisiacal. I raised my glass toward them and they joined in the toast.

Without them noticing, I took a picture of them and sent it to Allegra, who responded immediately: *Who is that with the Maestro? I can't wait to come to Milan!!!!!*, and when I asked her if she also had a little desire to see me, or only Vezzosi, she answered: *But certainly I also want to see you!* and attached a red heart, which I noted, however, was not beating.

When we left the restaurant we were all three a little tipsy, and on seeing Milena's Vespa parked out front, Vezzosi turned red and said that maybe we had better take a taxi, and then she looked at him for a second, smiled, and nodded, and when we were on our way to the hotel, Vezzosi told us about this guy Klein who was devoted to Saint Rita of Cascia, *the patron saint of impossible and desperate cases*, and he left her at the convent some *ex votos* with *a gold leaf, his blue and his pink*, and Milena and I looked at each other and burst out laughing because we had no idea what the fuck he was talking about. We said good-bye in the lobby. They, said Vezzosi, were going to stay down another five minutes and have something to drink at the hotel bar.

I went up to my room, wrecked, and just barely was able to collapse on the bed, where I fell asleep fully dressed. I heard a knock on the door and got up. It was him, in his bathrobe, agitated as hell.

"Zapata, give me a Viagra."

"Huh? What?"

"I need a Viagra right away, or a Cialis, whatever you have."

"What are you talking about ... Viagra? I don't have any Viagra."

He came in the room and sat down on the bed, his head in his hands.

"Well then, it's over. . . Mother Mary, it's over."

"What's happening?"

He raised his eyes to stare at me. He was desperate.

"It's happening that there are some problems, Zapata; some big problems . . . I'm too much involved, too much . . ."

"But what happened?"

"It happened that we kissed each other, and it was an enormous, immense, indescribable emotion, okay? . . . And then she took her clothes off, and on seeing her naked, I broke down . . . I broke down in tears because she is so beautiful . . . I like her more than when she was eighteen, believe me . . . She is an absolute wonder, because she's . . . she's more beautiful now, more true . . . It's her. The true Milena."

"And so?"

"And so, I can't get a hard-on, Zapata . . ."

"No?"

"No, nothing doing, Zapata. Zero. I don't know why, it's never happened to me. Maybe I'm too agitated, too nervous, I don't know . . . I don't know what it is . . . It can't be because of the drugs because by now the effect has worn off . . . Maybe it was the wine . . . Or maybe I love her too much to fuck her, what can I tell you . . . Maybe I just have to love her at a distance . . . I mean I never fucked her when we were kids, maybe it's not in the cards . . . But no, no, no . . . it can't end like this . . . Help me, Zapata, please, help me . . ."

"What should I do?"

"Call the desk and ask if they have any Vi-Viagra and ha-have it brought up to the room. I'll wa-wa-wait for you in the ba-ba-bathroom."

He was desperate, really totally desperate. A few minutes more and he would start to shake and he would go into a panic attack, like Mamadou had said, but I didn't have his medicine, and so I would really have to call the reception desk, to have them bring me some Xanax, not Viagra, and even in the best of cases, that is, if they actually had it and brought it to him right away, it would still have been a tragedy because then there'd be no way he'd get a hard-on, and so long to the evening out and so long to his pride and so long to Milena... So long to everything...

He put his hands over his face and started to moan, and I realized that the life of this man—but of every man, including my own—was nothing more than an infantile, furious, grotesque, blind journey toward disaster, and nothing that he had thought, and said and done and experienced up to that moment—much less the book that he had written—could save him in that moment.

Only I could save him.

And I did.

I grabbed him by the shoulders and said:

"Vezzosi, listen to me... Oh, Vittorio, look at me..."

He stopped moaning and raised his eyes. They were empty, glassy.

"Now, I'm going to tell you a secret. It's something nobody knows. The only one who knew it was my father, but he's no longer here, and so I'm going to tell it to you . . . Vezzosi, look at me, oh . . ."

He turned his head slowly toward me.

"I'm a virgin."

"Really?"

I nodded.

"What? With your girlfriend you've never . . . ?"

"Forget about my girlfriend, who anyway isn't my girlfriend anymore . . . Let's talk about Milena, and if I can allow myself to speak freely . . ."

He was looking me without seeing me.

"Oh, Vezzosi, are you there?"

"Yes."

"Listen to me. Can I speak freely or not?"

"Sure."

"So, I'm a virgin, okay? But I like women a lot. I'm crazy about them. I lose my head over women. And you have to know that your Milena is not only the most beautiful woman I've ever seen in my life, but also the most . . . yeah . . . the most pornographically desirable . . ."

Now he was staring at me.

"And I've seen plenty of them, Vezzosi, believe me, lots . . . I have an encyclopedic knowledge of the subject . . . Sure, not in person, unfortunately, only on my computer . . . But I can assure you that . . . That is, if I can continue to speak freely, I mean...Yeah, I already know that I'll beat off over her for the rest of my life..."

A spark lit up in the back of his eyes.

"Really? Because for me, she is a Madonna..."

"But what Madonna, Vezzosi...Take a good look at her. No, take a better look at her. She's a woman, that one, a real woman. Those eyes, those tits, the legs, the ass...I am certain that she goes to the gym every day...She's an absolute babe, the mother of all MILFs..."

He stared at me, surprised and pleased.

"The mother of all MILFs?"

"Yes, Vezzosi. And at this point, I'm going to confess something else to you."

"What?"

"Before falling asleep a little while ago, I gave myself a hand job over her..."

"No."

"Yes."

"Really?"

Yeah. I imagined I was humping her from behind, you know...With my hands grabbing her love handles and she turned around to look at me and was loving it...And then, in the end, she got down on her knees in front of me and took it in her hands and I came in her face.

His face turned to stone.

"Do it for me, Vittorio, come on...Go back up there and slam her all night, fuck. Do it for me and for everyone like

me, who will never find themselves in bed with someone like
Milena all their lives…"

He jumped to his feet, and for a minute I thought he was
going to jump down my throat, but then he offered me his hand.

"You're right, Zapata. Thanks a million."

We shook hands.

"You're a genius."

"Yeah, right."

"No, no, I know what I'm talking about… You're an absolute genius," he said again, and walked out of the room.

I threw myself back on the bed and fell asleep right away,
only to wake up when I heard someone pounding on the door
as if they wanted to break it down. I hadn't closed the curtains
and the light of dawn was lighting up the room. There he was
again at the door, still in his bathrobe, beaming. He gave me
such a bear hug he picked me up off the floor.

"Thank you, Zapata, thank you! It was a sweet as ambrosia,
as mead. And without you I never could have done it… Naturally, this is a secret to take to the grave, don't forget… But I
owe it all to you, everything, everything! What a mind blow,
what a triumph! It was a thousand times better than bonking a
twenty-year-old… A transcendent experience… And I turned
in a pretty good performance myself, I must say. Nothing epic,
but I got the job done!"

He took my face in his hands.

"What a day this has been, eh? Say it to me. It's worth an
entire lifetime! I was born to live days like this one, and you,

too! Because, always remember this, Zapata, our lives as men are short and dirty, a sea of shit and boredom and tragedies, but there are also some glorious moments, every once in a while. Isn't that true? Tell me, Zapata, isn't that true?"

And I, my cheeks squeezed together in his grip:

"Yes, Vezzosi, it's true!"

He turned and bounded out of the room, shouting:

"Life is good, life is sweet!"

I closed the doors, the curtains, and collapsed once again on the bed.

Money

• • •

I WAS DREAMING about my dad. We were playing tennis on a cliff-top court, overlooking the sea, dressed in white, with wooden rackets, and beneath us were whales spraying their enormous spouts. Then the bedside telephone rang.

"We're got to leave right away, Zapata, the fucking TV people are coming, and I don't want them to find me here. I'm downstairs waiting for you. Hurry up."

I staggered around the room, picking up my stuff, went out of the hotel, and found him waiting for me in the Jeep, the engine running. He had put on a baggy linen shirt over the usual jeans and square-toed boots.

"Come on, Zapata, run!"

We took off like a rocket, and as soon as we turned onto a wide boulevard, we were flanked by a black Fiat 500. At the passenger window, there was a really skinny guy in a T-shirt and vest, with dark glasses and short hair, and the word MONEY on his forehead.

"Look at that, Zapata, this jerk's got a tattoo on his face…"

I leaned out to look at him, and I saw him pull out a cell phone and point it at us. Then he shouted:

"Maestro! Maestro!"

"Who the hell is it?" Vezzosi said, and looked at me. I shrugged. A road vlogger. We should have expected it.

"Won't you say hi, Maestro?"

"Who are you? What do you want?"

"Give me the finger, come on!"

Money gave the thumbs-up like Fonzie.

"What do you want. Go away. I don't know you."

The black 500 stayed side by side with the Jeep, hiccupping its way along, constantly accelerating and braking. From the noise it made, it must have been a souped-up Fiat Abarth.

"Maestro Vezzosi, give me the finger. Come on!"

We had practically blocked the traffic in the two lanes of the boulevard, and car horns were already blasting from the cars in line behind us.

"This guy is drugged as pork roast… Go stick it up your ass," Vezzosi shouted at him, but Money was now sitting on the car door so he could record him better with the telephone. If he fell, he was sure to be crushed to death.

"Tell me to stick it up my ass again, Maestro, please… I didn't get a good shot…"

Vezzosi looked at me.

"What did he say?"

And then the 500 got so close that the two cars were touching, we heard a loud thud, and Vezzosi screamed:

"Fuck you doing, asshole?"

He swerved instinctively toward their car, which lurched right and banged up against the curb, went up on the sidewalk, crossed it, and went into a flower bed, where it stopped, leaning against a hedge. Vezzosi slowed down to see if anyone was hurt, but the concert of car horns turned deafening and we had to move on, while Money got out of the car limping and kept on filming us with his cell phone.

"Thank you, Maestro!" he was shouting, "Thank you!"

"Who was that nut, Zapata? What's going on? Who was that? He can't be one of my readers…"

"I haven't the slightest idea," and I shrugged my shoulders.

I took a look at my phone to see what had happened during the night, and was horrified to see that it had zero charge. I'd forgotten to charge it, and it was dead, finished. A stone.

I'd been unreachable for hours and hours, and by this time Allegra was supposed to have arrived in Milan without my being able to accompany her with messages during the journey, comfort her for getting up so early, ask her if the train was full, if her seat was facing forward like she preferred, if there was someone funny and friendly or unfriendly in her car, screaming children, dogs, imbeciles shouting into their telephones… And the tickets! Fuck, what did Allegra do about the tickets? She'd even brought some friends with her. Three! Who was going to give me the tickets, now?

I put my hands in my hair. What had happened to me? I was really out of control, if I couldn't even remember to keep my phone charged… Evidently, I liked it, then, playing the part of the passenger on the glorious journey... The young kid with no opinions or scruples, the nurse without medicines, the drunken lap-dance poet, the weathervane, the turncoat, the nouveau drug enthusiast, the privileged spectator of a show who spied cowardly on behalf of others behind the back of the protagonist, the man to whom I hadn't even dreamed of telling that half of Italy was deliriously watching him dive headfirst into an adventure that seemingly made no sense and had no end, the wild man who drove his open 1979 Jeep at breakneck speed down the streets of Milan, powered by a 6600 cc engine that consumed more gas than a Formula 1 race car and emitted the carbon dioxide of a fighter jet on takeoff, unaware of everything but calm, utterly calm, and happy because he was fresh from the most wonderful night of his life and couldn't wait to see his girlfriend again, and life and the world must have finally looked to him as they had looked when he was a teenager—a clean slate, or no, a blank page—and who managed, who knows how, to avoid pedestrians, pigeons, scooters, and all the streetcars whose tracks he insisted on following, in a mad race, as though he were driving an ambulance, because the other cars in front of us, many of which were hybrids or electric vehicles, swerved this way and that to let us pass as though they were alive, and our prey, terrorized on seeing in their rearview mirrors a monstrous phantasm out of the past, the most ferocious of predators from a savage bygone age, incalculably harsher and crueler and freer than today.

"What's up, Zapata? Everything okay?"

I told him everything.

About the meeting with Mamadou, the pact with Passini, the pictures, the Archangel, the internet posts, the ten thousand people who were waiting for him at the fair, the live TV and radio coverage on the web.

Everything.

Even the book of Epictetus that I'd stolen from him. Even my uncharged telephone. Even about Allegra and that I didn't know where she was and that she didn't have tickets to see him.

And he smiled and said he knew. He knew it all. He had always known everything and it didn't matter at all to him.

"I guess I'm old-fashioned, Zapata, but really, the fundamental significance of all that bullshit escapes me... Let's think instead about the important things. Would you like to have a nice breakfast of champions?"

I shook my head.

"Okay. Then let's go."

And he accelerated again.

Ragnarok,
from Morning Till Night

. . .

WHEN WE GOT to the fair, Milena was there waiting for us at a side entrance, with the jeans from the night before and a denim shirt with mother-of-pearl buttons and blue-logo Nike tennis shoes that must have been thirty years old.

She was splendid.

When she saw me, she lowered her eyes and I wondered if Vezzosi had told her about our conversation, but I told myself no, it was impossible, and meanwhile she escorted us through the enormous almost-empty pavilion, populated only by exhibitors busy giving the final touches to their stands as they waited for the visitors, who were still not to be seen, but who were undoubtedly numerous and very close and happy, mixed together with the audience of Vezzosi's followers, because we could hear them singing in chorus the words of a festive song that came blasting out of the loudspeakers at full volume, and repeated in English that *everybody has a hungry heart*.

Vezzosi started in right away saying wow here and wow there and roaming the stands, and I begged Milena to help me find some place to charge my phone. She led me into a small office with a leather armchair and a desk, behind which there was, sprawled on a chair fiddling with his iPhone, a fiftyish guy in a light blue jacket, white shirt, and jeans, his hair slicked back with gel. She introduced him to me as her husband, she told him I was Professor De Vito and bent over to plug in my cell phone to an outlet while he stared at me with a smile that put me off.

"So you're Zapata..."

"I guess so...Excuse me, just for a second, I've got to download some important messages..."

"Great job you've done, my boy, congratulations...You've showed him up big-time..."

He winked at me and went back to tapping the screen of that enormous iPhone that starting ringing just then, so loudly that we jumped, all three of us.

"Sweetheart," he answered, "good morning...Are you here already?"

He signaled us to leave the office. I started to say:

"I just need a second, I'm sorry, time to turn it on..."

But he repeated more intensely that gesture that struck me as infinitely discourteous and vulgar, so much so that I've never done it to anyone in my life—the one with the fingers closed pointing downward and the hand rotating from the wrist to indicate the direction to move in order to get yourself immediately out of someone's hair—and we left.

Milena pulled an embarrassed smile.

"It'll be just a few minutes, Emiliano, don't worry...But where's Vittorio?"

I pointed out a small group of people huddled together.

"He must be over there. Did I really show him up?"

She gave me a half smile.

"I don't know, Emiliano. It depends."

"On what?"

"On how it turns out."

We made our way over to him, passing through the stands, which were overflowing with a conglomeration of colorful and badly conserved stuff that looked like it had been dug out of recycling bins and scattered randomly on the counters.

There was a little of everything, of every shape, style, and color: jeans, shirts, caps, pants, T-shirts, down vests, sweatshirts, bathing suits, overcoats, jackets, vests, leather jackets, hooded coats, skirts, miniskirts, fur coats, gym shoes, scarves, boots, belts, socks, necklaces, neck-chains, bracelets, rings, earrings, perfumes, pins, eyeglasses, sunglasses, reading glasses, ski goggles, welder's glasses and pilot's goggles, adding machines, typewriters, cameras, Polaroids, binoculars, Walkmans, turntables, CD players, movie cameras, projectors, recorders, video recorders, synthesizers, equalizers, amplifiers, pre-amps, speakers, megaphones, walkie-talkies, football and rugby balls, tennis and Ping-Pong balls, baseballs and billiard balls, beach balls, buckets, shovels, molds, skis, sleds, saucer sleds, toboggans, golf clubs, baseball bats, tennis rackets (wood and metal), Ping-Pong paddles, ski poles, pool sticks, racing bikes and cross-country bikes, tricycles, pinball games, jukeboxes, license plates, restaurant and storefront signs, a gas pump with GULF written on the front.

And then books, hundreds of books, and vinyl records, piles and piles and piles of records, even the little 45s, magazines, journals, newspapers, graphic novels, sticker books, comic books, mountains of comic books, board games, advertising stickers, cash registers, cigarette cartons, plastic and glass ashtrays, lighters, cigar boxes, pens, crayons, colored pencils, lead pencils, pencil sharpeners, highlighters, pocket knives, floppy discs, audiocassettes, videocassettes, telephone cards, Nutella jars, wine bottles, liquor bottles, bottles of Coca-Cola.

And then transistor radios with straps, portable colored plastic TVs with round antennas, gray plastic tabletop telephones, the earliest computers, the first Game Boys. And then, Vespas and scooters, sure, naturally. And cars, lots of cars. And one stand that had only small trucks with the OM trademark.

It was all used. Old stuff. Scratched, faded, torn, stained, cracked, full of holes, dented, chipped, threadbare, or else waxed and polished as shiny as possible, respected, maybe even loved, and displayed as a single, immense relic.

I asked myself who were these people who treated as treasures all that junk, and what must have happened to them to choose to live with their heads facing backwards like the soothsayers in the *Divine Comedy*, and I felt sorry for them.

But why do I always feel sorry for everybody, eh?

"Oh, there they are...Did you get lost? Milena, look at those beautiful T-shirts. Could you ask that gentleman if he would sell me the TWA? Ah, it's not for sale? What a drag...And the Pan Am? Fuck, is this a fair or a museum?"

The exhibitor—a short, bald guy with bright eyes, the shadow of a beard, and a white shirt with a blue collar—picked up the T-shirt and walked over to Vezzosi.

"They're not for sale for you, Vittorio, and you know why? Because as rich as you are, you don't have enough money to buy these T-shirts...For people like you and me these things are priceless, and so..."

He held them out to him.

"You can only accept them as a gift...my gift."

Vezzosi was left speechless and, instead of shaking the little guy's hand, hugged him.

"Thanks a million, brother."

"No, thanks a million to you, Vittorio. Your book changed my life..." the exhibitor said, slipping out of the hug, his bright eyes having become teary. "What the hell are two T-shirts..."

Vezzosi smiled, turned the T-shirts over to Milena, and went on his way in procession, followed and welcomed by the smiles and adoring gazes of the exhibitors of both sexes who couldn't take their eyes off him, while the ten thousand outside were singing in chorus, in English, that they were *born in the USA*, and I took advantage of the swelling crowd of followers to peel away and run back to the office, because by that time the cell phone must have recharged enough to get it up and running.

When I walked in, Milena's husband was still talking, but I detached the phone from the outlet and turned it on right in front of him as he frantically signaled me to go away, with his scowl getting grimmer by the second. I ignored him, while I stared at the screen that was coming on. Some time ago, I thought, or rather, some days ago—it wouldn't have gone like this. I would have recoiled, intimidated, and I would have left the office. Now, no. So, it had been useful for something, the *cursus honorum*. When he flipped me the finger, I smiled at him, reciprocated, and walked out.

There were tons of unanswered calls, almost all from Allegra, but also from Mama, Passini, Monnanni, Mamadou, and a landline in Milan. There were dozens of messages, too. I checked the ones from Allegra first. They said that she had boarded the train, that she was so happy about today, that she had arrived in Bologna, that she was coming into Milan, that she had arrived in Milan and wanted to know where we should meet, that she didn't understand why I didn't turn on my phone, that anyway she was on her way to the fair, that she had arrived at the fair and didn't know what to do because she didn't have tickets, that she was pissed because she was outside the gate with her three friends and I wasn't answering, that she didn't understand what was going on, that this was no way to behave, and anyway, where the fuck was I...

I ran to Vezzosi to tell him that we had to let Allegra in right away, that she was waiting outside, and he jokingly wrinkled his brow and asked me if I was sure her name was Allegra because I had always spoken to him about a certain Alice, but when he saw that I was desperate, he smiled and explained the thing to Milena, who called someone and ordered that they let in *immediately* a girl named Allegra, or Alice, who was outside the gates with three friends, and on the other end this someone must have made some objection, because she repeated the whole thing word by word, while Vezzosi shouted that if Allegra or Alice and all of her friends weren't let in, he wasn't opening his mouth and was going straight back to Florence.

"Which gate, Emiliano? There are a lot of them."

I called her.

"Ciao, Allegra."

"Ciao, my ass! Now you answer me?"

"I'm sorry, but this morning has been really crazy…"

"You're telling me, I got up at dawn to get here and be locked out…"

"No, come on, they're coming to get you."

"No, look, forget it, this is impossible. They'll never be able to find me in this chaos. You can't imagine how many people are here. It's absolute insanity…I'll listen to him talk from out here, if possible, if not, the hell with it."

"No, no. Wait…"

"I know you tried…but you couldn't do it…like always…"

"Allegra, give me a break…"

Milena asked me:

"Which gate is it? Have her tell you which gate it is…"

"Thanks just the same, anyway, Emiliano, really…And don't worry that I got up before the crack of dawn and came three hundred kilometers for nothing, just because you told me I could come and that you would get me in because you're a friend of Vezzosi, no, a close friend. Everything's fine, really, thanks again…"

"Which gate are you at?"

"Gate four, goddamn it! I'm at gate four."

"She's at four, Milena. At gate four."

"Okay, I'll go. Show me what she looks like, this Allegra…"

"Don't go anywhere, Milena's coming to get you. Now hang up, I have to show her what you look like…"

She went on:

"What's that supposed to mean, what I look like? Emiliano, what are you saying?"

I showed a picture of her to Milena, who looked at it for a few seconds, and then stared at me.

"What is it?"

"No, nothing…"

She walked off looking like a queen, while a group of exhibitors, having gotten their courage up to approach him, had gathered around Vezzosi, many of them carrying his book. One young woman said she was from RAI TV, and Vezzosi announced that naturally he wouldn't be giving any interviews to anybody, but for whatever they wanted to know, they should talk to *Professor De Vito*, pointing to me, and as four of them crowded around me calling me Professor here and Professor there, my phone rang again.

"Allegra, Milena is on her way..."

"Who's Allegra? What in the world?... So, finally you deign to respond, eh? Good for you, Emiliano, really...Anyway, let me tell you right away that you're fired, because this is no fucking way to act, damn it. I've called you a thousand times, since yesterday, and you never answered. You haven't even answered the Archangel's calls, so who do you think you are, eh? You let all this go to your head, young fella?"

I heard the voice of Monnanni interjecting.

"No, Passini! Hold on! What are you saying!"

"Stop it, you fool! Let go of the phone..."

"Why would he help you if you fire him, you imbecile...Let me talk to him, give me the phone...Emiliano, don't take it the wrong way, forgive him. He's hysterical this morning, and plus he's agoraphobic...Three people around him is enough to make him go on tilt..."

"What are you talking about? I'm not agoraphobic. Give me the phone."

"He's very tense, poor guy, very agitated, and actually so am I, Emiliano, but let's get beyond that...Don't pay attention to what he just said to you: for sure you're not fired, I can guarantee you that...We know very well that the time and ways of an artist cannot be those of an accountant, and that his heart lives in perpetual tumult, and he doesn't have and cannot have masters..."

"Who the hell is the accountant? What the fuck are you saying, Monnanni? And he isn't an artist, this guy. If anyone is, it's the other one. I'm saying, if anyone..."

"Shut up! Keep your mouth shut! I was saying, Emiliano, that we know well, we high-ranking scholars, that an artist cannot live the entire day attached to this vulgar talking cup..."

"What's with all this touchy-feely crap, damn it! Ask him where they are! Make him tell you where they are!"

"I'm here with him, Professor. Tell that to Passini. And tell him to please calm down, too. Otherwise, I'm hanging up right away."

"Sure, Emiliano, right away. I'll tell him right now. You're right. Could you please shut up, eh? You want to keep quiet or not? You're exacerbating things for no use! You're going to ruin everything...Look, Arrighetti is almost here, go to him. Let me talk to Emiliano..."

"Tell him, though, about the announcement, if not, the whole thing goes up in smoke, understand?"

"Yeah, I'll tell him. Now go, go!...So, Emiliano, listen...Have patience and forgive him, these are tough times...We came to Milan on a horrendous nineteenth-century military transport train to save a few cents, surrounded by shouting tourists... *O tempora! O mores!* But now we're here, and even though we've been bounced around by this barbaric and already drunk mob singing totally incomprehensible Anglo-Saxon anthems, well, Emiliano, we need to talk to Vittorio...urgently. Is he there with you?"

Surrounded by journalists and exhibitors, in front of a stand about ten meters from me, Vezzosi was brandishing a glass bottle, full of a white liquid:

"Look, you guys, this is almond milk...You would put two fingers of it in the glass and then add water...But what's that, grenadine? No, wow, that stuff is serious...Even if grenadine used to give me the shits because it was too sweet, and you, no?"

They were in adoration. They drank down every word he said. A German journalist asked the exhibitor how to spell *grenadine*.

"Yes, Professor Monnanni, certainly."

"Okay...because here with us there is also Doctor Arrighetti, from the publishing house, and he would very much like to say hello to him and exchange a few words in private, before the *lectio magistralis*. Just a few words, but very important, believe me. Could you let me talk to him?"

"Right now, I think that's a little complicated, Professor."

"Couldn't you try?"

"It's not a good moment, believe me..."

"But do you at least know what he's going to say? Is he going to talk about the new novel? Because that would really be a great idea and it would take care of everything, you know what I mean? Tell that to Vittorio. All he has to do is announce

the release of the new novel, and all of the misunderstand-
ings will be erased...All the doubts, all the arguments, all the
anger, all the economic problems for everybody would van-
ish instantly...His, too, tell him that...He'd fix himself up
for life, and he wouldn't have to give up anything...Doctor
Arrighetti, who is right here next to me, and who is a most
trustworthy person, understands the situation perfectly...He
realizes that the relationship Vittorio has with his readers
is unique in all the world, there is a true blazing love between them...What? Ah, yes, of course...Excuse me, Emiliano...What's that, Doctor Arrighetti?"

Vezzosi shouted:

"No, even tamarind? I can't believe it...Tamarind gave me
the shits, too, I have to say, but I got off on the name a lot..."

And everybody laughed.

"Ta-ma-rin-do!" he shouted.

"So, Emiliano, Doctor Arrighetti authorizes me to say
that he is ready to offer immediately a very significant ad-
dendum for the second novel, and to sign a new contract for
the third. Yes...At the conditions established by Vittorio, he
tells me...All he has to do is announce the release of the new
novel for September or October. Even November is all right,
in any case before Christmas...Tell him right now, Emiliano,
please...Emiliano? Are you there, Emiliano?"

I turned to look at Vezzosi, who was explaining to his
audience that for the Babylonians the tamarind was a sacred
plant that drove away evil spirits. I gestured to him, but he

didn't see me, and the television crew, thinking that their moment had arrived, crowded around me and started back in, asking me if Vezzosi could speak after the event, if he would be giving interviews, if he could do a live radio feed, if there was a press release already available, if in the afternoon there would be time to do something a little longer...

"Emiliano, hello...Emiliano..."

I could hear the crackling voice of Monnanni, and then finally Vezzosi turned and came toward me, fending off the gathering of the faithful. He took me under his arm and announced, as dozens of photos were being snapped:

"Excuse me, guys, but now I need a minute of calm with Professor De Vito, before going out there...Anyway, we'll see each other later. There's a press conference already scheduled, no?"

A volley of shouts. Where? When? How long? Here? Who's going to be there?

"I don't know! Contact the press office! For now, that's enough! Please!" he shouted, "Get the hell out of here, all of you!"

It worked.

They stopped, speechless, for a few seconds, and he and I went back up the line of stands that they had just come down.

"Where can we go, Zapata? In a minute they'll start following us again. Isn't there a dressing room?"

"There's the office of Milena's husband."

"In fact, I've got to have a word with that guy...Who's on the phone. Passini?"

I handed him the phone.

"Sauro, ciao. It's Vittorio, how's it going? No, he hasn't told me anything yet…Now. I'll talk to him…No, but what Ragnarok: come on, everything's going fine…No, him, I don't want to talk to. I'm not talking to him…No…"

And then there was a long pause, during which Vezzosi listened and nodded.

"Ah," he kept repeating: "Ah…Ah…"

He turned to look at me.

"I got it. Okay. What I'm going to say you'll be able to hear in about ten minutes…Oh, by the way, Sauro, I heard about the happy event, congratulations! So, it still works, that old wrinkly pipette of yours…Bravo, for God's sake, bravo!"

He hung up and we went into the office. Milena's husband jumped to his feet and came right toward me with his finger raised. He put it under my nose.

"When I tell you to get out of my office, you leave, okay? You got that, jerk-off?"

"Where the fuck do you get off?" Vezzosi said.

"And you, what do you want? Who the fuck are you?"

"I'm the one who's here to save your ass, dumb shit. I'm the one they're waiting for, the thousands of them, out there."

And there was this incredibly long pause, during which these overweight fifty-year-olds, more or less the same height—the same color and the same length of hair, the same white linen shirt—looked at each other straight in the eye a few inches apart like two marble lions, their paunches nearly touching.

"And I'm also the one who today takes Milena and carries her away."

On the face of the husband a mean smile formed.

"I really don't think so."

"But yes. Because you don't deserve her, dickhead."

"Neither do you, sleazeball."

Vezzosi gave him a push on the chest, and the husband pushed back, and then Vezzosi went for him and I put myself between them, but I'm short and above my head I could hear a great smacking of hands, and in the meantime, I took a bunch of elbows to the head from both of them.

"Stop! Stop!" I said, but them, nothing.

"She's a whore, anyway, if you really want to know, she's a goddam floozy bitch and that's it…" the husband yelled. And Vezzosi:

"I'll kill you! Swear to God, I'll kill you…"

They started throwing punches and I was still there in the middle and then someone stumbled, maybe me, and all three of us fell down. They started wrestling, pulling each other by the hair and grabbing their shirts, and Vezzosi's ripped and he cursed and grabbed Milena's husband's shirt at the chest and the buttons went flying like bullets and one hit me in the eye and I yelped in pain and then they stopped, and for a minute there was silence because, despite all the fracas, the only one to get hurt was me, with my vision in my right eye now blurred, and I said it, and then Vezzosi took my face in his hands and took a look at my eye and said it was nothing, it was just a little red, but he didn't have his glasses and so he couldn't be sure, and he blamed it on Milena's husband, who instead protested that it had been Vezzosi, who had ripped off his shirt and sent the buttons flying, so it was his fault, and then he examined my eye and said that there was nothing wrong but meanwhile I had started to tear up, and on seeing me cry, Vezzosi got infuriated and grabbed Milena's husband by what was left of his shirt and started shaking him really hard, and at that moment Milena walked into the office with Allegra and each put a hand in front of her mouth and the three of us froze.

"Ten minutes and you're on live TV," she said, "I've got nothing else to say."

And she walked out of the office pulling Allegra behind her.

They tried to get themselves back together but you could see they'd had a scuffle. Their hair was all messed up, the husband had a black eye, and Vezzosi had a scratch on his cheek. Their shirts were ready to be thrown away. Milena came back in and tossed the TWA and Pan Am T-shirts at them. Allegra looked at me, incredulous.

"Put these on, alpha males..."

They put them on in silence—Vezzosi took the TWA—and the five of us walked out of the office. As we were walking down the aisle, the exhibitors lined up on either side as we passed, and applauded.

Buy Them!
Take Them Home!

. . .

"THIS MILENA, WHO is she?" whispered Allegra, who was walking alongside me. "Because I just reread on the train that piece where the protagonist describes his girlfriend, and she's dressed like that. I mean the same identical...the denim shirt with mother-of-pearl buttons, the Nikes...It's her, right? It's her after all this time? Oh, Emiliano, Milena is the leading lady of *The Wolves Inside*, right? Tell me, come on..."

We walked out through an emergency exit and we were struck by the sunlight and the heat and the noise and by the immense force of those thousands of invisible people who were about thirty meters away from us, beyond the black drapes of the stage set.

The music had been interrupted and all you could hear was a sort of constant roar while two young hostesses in suits guided us up the stairs of the stage that was actually the stage for the singers, with the metal scaffolding to hold up the lighting way up high, the black drapes in the role of wings, and the floor of polished resin all scratched, and then one of the drapes moved because of the wind and for a second we glimpsed that enormous crowd of people that looked like a colored sea, and my heart leapt to my throat from the emotion, followed immediately by the relief that it was not me who had to speak in front of all those people, but we were already passing between two behemoths in black T-shirts and camouflage pants, and entering the backstage, that was a small space furnished with plastic chairs and a table laid out with a tray of fruit, a dozen bottles of water, and an ice bucket, with the neck of an open bottle of champagne sticking out of it.

There were already about ten people backstage with glasses in hand: young men and women sparkling with necklaces and rings and enormous watches. As soon as they saw us, they went silent and started staring at Vezzosi, who was immediately approached by a guy holding up a telephone and suddenly we heard the roar of the crowd, because positioned on one of the chairs was a monitor that was evidently sending the image from the phone to some giant screen, and there, in a close-up, was Vittorio.

With a two-day-old beard, his salt-and-pepper hair down to his shoulders, and the TWA T-shirt, he looked like some movie version of himself, a famous actor who was playing him in a film about his life, and maybe he even noticed this thing because a big smile of amusement appeared on his face as the frame opened out to show his tattooed arms and his jeans with a hole at the knee and the square-toed boots, and then, even me standing next to him, a short, overweight, clean-shaven young guy, with already thinning hair and white short-sleeved shirt full of wrinkles who was staring at the camera with the eyes of a surprised puppy.

I saw myself swallow from the emotion, then Vezzosi made a sign to someone from security—a fortysomething with a crew cut and mirror glasses who looked like a soldier and made me scared just to look at him—and whispered something in his ear. The guy nodded, said, *Sure, Maestro*, and politely asked the young guy with the cell phone and all the other elegant people to leave, *now*. Only in that moment, an instant before Allegra muttered it to me, did I notice that among all those people with the glasses of champagne in hand, there was also Carlita Cosmay.

Milena's husband said that it was impossible, they were his guests, but Vezzosi stared at him and put his index finger on his lips, and the other snapped into action and started managing with big smiles and vague promises, the immediate exit of Carlita and her entourage, among which I recognized a famous model of lingerie, two rappers in baggy shirts, and the center forward from the national football team, who raised a timid protest, but the behemoth from security proclaimed: *Right now the Maestro needs a moment of total concentration*, and he accompanied them outside to the oceanic applause of the audience, that saw and heard the whole scene and enjoyed it enormously. Then the giant turned toward the young guy who was filming him and gestured to him, too, to get out of there.

"Emiliano, ciao, I'm Gabriel, the Archangel..." he said without shutting off the camera. "Tell him I'm working..."

They all turned to look at me, but I didn't know what to say or do, so Vezzosi intervened:

"You sure didn't choose such a great name, you know? When it comes right down to it, the archangel Gabriel was a dickhead, a sort of hit man... He was the one who sent that rain of fire down on those poor sodomites... Out, out, you too, get out."

The colossus took a step toward the Archangel, who interrupted the video and approached Vezzosi with his right hand outstretched:

"Anyway, you are one of the greats, Vezzosi, let me tell you..."

"You, on the other hand, are not, let me tell you."

While they were shaking hands, the Archangel smiled and gave me a wink, then he left the backstage followed by the giant, and those left were me, Vittorio, Milena, Allegra, and Milena's husband, who was sitting on a chair with his hands in his hair and repeating that this was not the right way to do things.

Then Allegra hugged me and gave me a kiss. In all that chaos, we hadn't yet said hello.

"Emiliano," she said, "will you introduce me?"

Vezzosi was sitting with his back turned to everyone, on one of those director's chairs. He was munching on an apple and looking at the monitor showing the crowd outside. Milena was sitting on her haunches beside him with her hand on his arm without saying anything. I figured this was a good time, so I took Allegra by the hand, and I was about to go introduce her when, on the monitor, there appeared that famous young emcee, whom my mother likes so much because she says he is always so cheerful and polite, and from the loudspeakers we heard him greet the audience and explain how there was no need of an introduction for Vittorio Vezzosi, and that he, too, was one of his biggest fans—*Just like all of you*, he said to the crowd, who responded with a roar—and when he had heard that he was coming to Milan he had asked the organizer *on his knees* if he could be the one to welcome him, and now he couldn't wait to hear him speak, but first, however, he had to give the floor for a minute to *the visionary who had imagined and created SuperVintage19!, the biggest and most important Eighties and Nineties Market-Fair in the whole world, Franco Casamonti!*

We all turned to look at Milena's husband. He had gotten up on his feet, and he didn't have that cutting look on his face of before, when he threw me out of his office. He looked tense, nervous. He took a deep breath, exhaled, smoothed his hair back, and went out onto the stage with his light blue jacket, jeans, and the Pan Am T-shirt. On the monitor we saw him shake hands with the cheerful polite young emcee, and grab the microphone. Then he looked at the audience, cleared his throat, and started talking:

"Good afternoon and welcome to *SuperVintage19!*, that I have the pleasure and honor to have invented and organized from the very beginning... This is the tenth edition of our wonderful fair, the biggest and most complete ever, and I want to greet and thank right here and now all those viewers who are watching us on the web and on television and who are listening to us on the radio, the authorities, our sponsors, and above all our exhibitors, who continue to grow in numbers and in quality and now come from all over Europe... This year we also have the honor to welcome our first friends in stars and stripes, and I salute and welcome them, too! By now, we are the biggest event in Europe, no, in the world, in a sector that is in constant exponential growth everywhere... And really, how could it be any different? All of us, finally, are realizing that the 1980s and '90s were absolutely the best years in the history of mankind, and that the things invented and built in those fateful decades are the most beautiful of all time and make everything that is made today pale in comparison... Certainly, even in the 1960s and '70s some marvelous things were created, but they will be the object of the new, extraordinary market-fair that we will be inaugurating in November, right here as always, in this same location and I would like to issue an invitation right now for you to join us here, with all of your passion and all of your enthusiasm..."

The emcee moved closer to him, perhaps believing he had finished, but Casamonti stopped him cold with a glance and went on:

"You know what the secret of our success is? It's something really simple, almost banal. An unequivocal and absolute certainty...indisputable..."

He paused for a second, smiled.

"The old is better than the new! A thousand times better!"

From the audience came a rising murmur of approval, and then came a *Bravo!* that set off some islands of applause.

"The new just doesn't make it, it disappoints us every day... There's nothing to it, no flair, no joy, no genius, no elegance, no excess... It's sad and dreary stuff, without quality, that in order to please everybody, pleases no one... My friends, the new sucks..."

A brief applause.

"What a wonderful world it was, on the other hand, the one we grew up in! How incalculably distant from the shameful stagnation of today! Our world was so good we didn't even notice how good it was! It seemed normal to us that our standard of living was always growing, every day, for everybody... It seemed natural to us to live surrounded by beauty, in art, in design... Yes, because the Vespas and the Fiat 500s that we used every day to go to school and to work, today are on exhibit at the Museum of Modern Art in New York! They were art, first of all! But not only them... the television sets we sat in front of, the radios we listened to, even the refrigerators and the washing machines that we had in our homes, not to mention the furniture, the tables, the chairs, the lamps, the typewriters... Everything in our daily lives was art! Blue-collar workers went to the factory driving a work of art, do you ever think about that? Secretaries filled out the invoices of their companies on Olivetti typewriters that were works of art...It was a fantastic world...Never before in history had it happened that beauty was affordable for everybody, and not only for the rich! Never! Am I right or not?"

From the audience came a warm round of applause, but Casamonti started talking again, stifling it.

"And there wasn't only Made in Italy. There was Made in the USA, the American Dream, to drive us wild...Now, all of this is what you'll find here, at the stands of our exhibitors...From motorcycles to leather jackets, from Game Boys to T-shirts...everything. It's all here. All the things that we loved and still love. Look at them, touch them, caress them, remember them...You can even get emotional, without fear, because we understand each other, and no one will judge you, enjoy..."

He stopped for a second, smiled, and from the audience came a fresh round of applause, which this time, however, Casamonti let fade out before he started talking again.

"But then, buy the things that you like so much! Take it from me, buy them! Take them home with you! They cost very little but they have great value, and they will always be worth more, because they contain our stories, our lives, and so they will continue to grow in price...It's inevitable...It's not just a matter of collecting...We'll leave that to the rich and the know-it-alls...To the *maestri*...It's much more...It's re-finding ourselves...a coming back into contact with the best years of our lives...It's turning our backs on this world of horrible decadence, where houses aren't worth anything anymore and money doesn't get you anything anymore and so it's worth nothing...So buy back your past! Take it back for yourselves! Defend it from those who would erase it! It will be your best investment, believe me...Buy them today, the things that you see on exhibit, because next year they will cost more, and the year after still more...And you know why? Because they *are real*. They are *originals*.

He nodded and stopped for a second, enjoying the attention from the audience, and then went on:

"Make repairs, sure...No, *restore*...Because time weighs on and corrodes everything, if you don't fight it...But what can be bad about restoring things, eh?...We restore art, we restore beauty, what's ugly we throw away...Only the originals count in life, you know that...Not the artificial, not reproductions, not fakes...Not the obscene replicas that the multinationals would like to sell us, they, who are the first to blame for our decadence, because they have taken away our jobs and shipped them to China..."

The loudest applause exploded, during which the cheerful and polite emcee went back behind the wings, scared by hearing that attack on the multinationals whose advertisements financed his programs and his very life.

"And now, after all they have done...now they would like to sell us the perfect trap that they've built just for us...Yes, because these bastards have set out to imitate the beautiful things of our time, understand? The cars, and the motorcycles, and the scooters, and the jackets and the shoes and the clothes, everything... They make them in China and then they want to sell them to us... to us, who know and use and love the originals! To us that *made* the originals! They think we're imbeciles, apparently... people with rings in their noses, that don't recognize the fraud implicit in the very concept of the replica... But no! Let's tell them to their faces. No! We want the originals!"

More applause.

"And who cares if they have defects... Even better! If the Vespas, instead of braking, screeched to a halt. If the 500s were made of tin. If the Jeeps didn't hold the road. If your Clarks, when you played football in them, got torn apart... Even better! They had a soul! They were fragile, imperfect, like us! They got worn out, like us! They had to be taken care of, like us! We don't want products that are perfect, that don't have a soul. We don't give a damn about perfection, to us..."

Amid the uproarious applause, Vezzosi muttered to Milena:

"Listen to him... He's damn good..."

"We want... No, *we want again*... objects that are beautiful, because beauty is everything... Objects that you can be happy and even proud to wear... Objects that represent us and speak of us to the world... And don't come talking to us about what's new, about novelty! There isn't anything really new, by now, in the world, and for decades...Aside from Apple, because Steve Jobs was one of us and thought like we think, where is the new? It no longer exists. There are only updates of things that already existed...Oh, how I hate them, updates...corrections, fine-tunings...You know why things are that way? Because they're afraid of the new! They don't know how to do it anymore, and can't even imagine it! They're afraid to take risks. They're afraid to surprise the market, to disconcert their global fucking customers..."

He started to pretend to weep.

"And what if the Chinese get offended? And if they don't like it in Russia? And if there are protests in Saudi Arabia? Ah, go fuck yourselves, you and the Chinese, and the Russians and the Saudi Arabians!"

This set off an enormous applause, that took a while to simmer down.

"Because the new is impolite and tough, my friends, and sometimes you can't understand it right away. The new looks you in the eye and forces you to change your mind. It shocks you. It fucks with you. But they, the ones who have massacred us, those sons of bitches from the multinationals with their bureaucrat accomplices and their snooty professors...the ones who have stolen our future and our children's futures and thrown them down the toilet...They are afraid of the new, and so they make replicas of the old and tell us it's new. They tell us: '*Oh, guys, everything's okay, take it easy, there's nothing wrong...You feel like you're poor, but it's not true, the future is bright, take your cell phone out of your pocket and buy our replicas, and tomorrow we'll have them delivered to your door by our slaves…* Because they've bought themselves an army of slaves, damn them, and those slaves are our children… This, according to them, is the only work that's suitable for our children… delivery boys… No, no, here everything has got to change! Everything! We are millions, and they have to listen to us! Are we nostalgic? Yes! Sure! Of course! Because it was better before!"

Now intensifying the applause, and making it foreboding, there was a kind of gruesome grumbling. It was anger, and it scared me.

"It was better before!" Casamonti shouted. "It was better before! Certainly, it was better before! A thousand times better…"

And then his voice went hoarse.

"Get me a glass of water!" he barked, and from behind the wings a hostess immediately came running out to bring him a bottle of water that he drank from like football players do, pouring the water directly into his mouth without touching it with his lips.

Those few seconds of interruption were enough to sap his energy. When he took the microphone back from the hands of the hostess, Casamonti went adrift, looking out at that endless crowd who had relished his every word, and he was lost. He struggled to smile, but the sacred flame had gone out. He had already said it all, and a thousand times better than he had ever dreamed.

"Let's show them!" He tried to get back on track. "Let's stop buying their crap! Let's say no to this world without value and without a future! No, let's go back to the future!"

And then, as though disconcerted by this last, problematic invocation, he stopped and looked around, as if to implore the return of the cheerful and polite emcee, who arrived immediately with a little run and put an arm around his shoulders as he announced into the microphone:

"Ladies and gentlemen, the emperor of nostalgia, the great Franco Casamonti!"

The audience growled and started to applaud and kept on applauding as Casamonti kept on thanking them. He even hazarded an exhausted and relieved bow, with his hand squeezed tight around the microphone.

"But he's a phenomenal rabble-rouser," Vezzosi chimed in.

And Milena:

"In fact, he wants to get into politics … But he's never talked like this, Vittorio, I swear it … It must be you're being here, maybe he feels the competition …"

When the applause died out, Casamonti spoke again:

"Thank you, thank you, indeed … Now I'll leave you to our guest, Maestro Vezzosi, who has deigned to come out of his hermitage to come here to us because he is a childhood friend of my wife … When they were kids, they went to school together, and so when she asked him, he dropped everything and came running … Last night, I even let them go out to dinner together …"

He raised his eyebrows, and made a little smile.

"They had to talk to each other about when they were young, reading Catullus together... You know, they're a couple of intellectuals..."

A chill ran down my spine, *Catullus?* Allegra pursed her lips.

Casamonti spread his arms out wide, the audience smiled, and Vezzosi looked at Milena.

"Son of a bitch..." he whispered in admiration, while she didn't take her eyes off the monitor and kept on biting her lower lip.

The audience started rumbling, and the young cheerful and polite emcee quickly took back the microphone and took a few strides, leaving Casamonti motionless and mute, disarmed, at the center of the stage.

"Ah yes, but now the moment has arrived to *quiet down*, as he would say, and leave some space to the man who moved us twenty-five years ago and continues to move us today... and who moves our daughters and sons... And he will move our grandchildren with his unique, marvelous, perfect novel which has sold millions and millions of copies around the world, and from which two movies were made, and it seems that a Chinese remake is in the planning stages... I'm joking, Casamonti, not to worry... I'm sure I speak for everybody when I say that we are infinitely honored to have here today the silent prophet of our time, maybe even the spiritual father for many of us, who grew up with his book on our bedside table...He hasn't spoken in public for a lifetime, and today he has come to tell us of his and our wonderful 1980s and '90s, at least I think so...Right?"

He turned toward Casamonti, who shrugged his shoulders.

"Or maybe not. We don't know. Well, that's even better. It'll be a surprise. We don't know what he's going to talk to us about. He'll do as he likes, as indeed he has always done. Ladies and gentlemen, the king of kings, the last alpha male...Vittorio Vezzosi!"

Vezzosi stood up, turned to me, and said in a whisper:

"As soon as I've finished talking, we're out of here, Zapata. Be ready!"

And he climbed onto the stage.

The Last Ray

. . .

HE APPEARED ON the monitor offering a brief, begrudging smile to all those people who had leaped to their feet to applaud him, as the camera motors clicked and buzzed and the sound of stadium horns lacerated the air. Who knows if he saw them, the enraptured faces of the thousands of spectators acclaiming him as if he were a rock star, the placards with the hashtag #Iwanttodovezzosi, the sheet twenty meters long that slowly unraveled to reveal the script: I'VE NEVER BEEN SO HAPPY IN ALL MY LIFE.

"What's that supposed to mean?" I whispered to Allegra.

"It's the last sentence of *The Wolves Inside* ... I can't believe you still haven't read it ..."

Milena heard and she looked at me for a second, then she redirected her gaze to the monitor, where Vezzosi was still smiling without saying anything, immobile, and I asked myself what I should do if he got a panic attack right then and there, in front of half of Italy, even though Vezzosi actually seemed a long way off from a panic attack, and, on the contrary, looked like he was having a world of fun, all of that adoration...Maybe I hadn't understood him at all, not me nor anyone else...Maybe that's what he really wanted: adoration. Pure. Crystalline. No questions. That and only that.

He moved slowly toward the young emcee and took the microphone from his hands, then he stared at him and Casamonti for a second and they stepped backwards without saying a thing, disappearing into the wings. The monitor was filled by the tightest of close-ups. Practically all you could see were his eyes.

One, two, three seconds.

"Ciao," he said, and ten thousand answered him.

"But what's this bullshit about the fucking alpha male..." he said, turning toward the wings, and the audience laughed.

"I have no idea what I'm supposed to say, now...I haven't prepared anything...But I would stand here for a lifetime looking at you all, because between us there's no need for words. You know how things stand...You know who I am..."

An enormous applause. The camera closed in on a woman around fifty with red cheeks, who was already drying a teardrop.

"You look really good, though...You're in good shape, yeah, you really don't look so bad...Actually, to say it straight, we are not actually doing so bad...It could have gone worse, with all the time that's passed, right? And instead, we're still here...Alive, damn it, alive as hell..."

Another enormous applause.

"Anyway, thanks for coming…Really, thanks a lot."

He turned again toward the wings, touched his back, stretched his arms and legs.

"Ah, what a night…I'm totally wrecked…Reading Catullus was super strenuous, really…"

The director closed in on Casamonti, who turned white, and Vezzosi remained silent for a few seconds while the audience laughed.

"I'm joking, eh…But it's true that I came because Milena asked me to. I couldn't say no to her. That's impossible…It's not true that we went to school together, but it is true that when I was a kid, I fell madly in love with her. One of those terrifying crushes…total…invincible…But I didn't have the courage to go and talk to her about it, though, because, just like she is today, Milena was incredibly beautiful and I was really shy and afraid of just about everything, and so…"

He paused, waited for a few seconds.

"Anyway, I miss the '80s, too, and the '90s…which actually, though, were really different from one another, and you certainly can't lump them together like that guy did earlier…The 1980s are one thing and the 1990s are another thing, you all know that…And the objects were pretty, sure, very pretty…But what I miss about those years is not so much the objects…Partly, because I still have them. I kept them all. The Vespas, the Jeeps, the clothes, the boots…I go around and I wear them…You can see that, no?"

He pointed to the TWA T-shirt, the jeans, the boots.

"But, you know, they're objects, and objects count for what they are, not all that much...He has to sell them, and he has to talk like that, sure, but he was talking about something else, actually...That guy before wasn't really talking about objects, he was talking about the past, and he wanted it for himself...Restored, maybe...I understand that, sure...But one thing I've learned, in all these years...and that is that the past, there's no way to bring it back...Even Gatsby couldn't do it. You remember him, don't you? At some point, Nick says to him that you can't repeat the past, and he gets indignant and goes: *Can't repeat the past? Why, of course you can! I'm going to fix everything, just the way it was before. She'll see...*But he couldn't do it. And he was Gatsby, not Casamonti..."

A few nervous laughs violated the great silence, and Vezzosi repeated with a thin reed of a voice, as though he were lost in thought:

"Fix everything, just the way it was before..."

Then he raised his head and looked straight out at the audience.

"When we are kids, it seems like we will be kids forever, right? Every day counts, every day has weight. Every hour, every minute that goes by seems to dilate and aspire to contain it all, our whole life...And time never passes...And then, all of a sudden, you're thirty and you're in your car, and on the radio, they're playing a song you used to like and you find yourself remembering how you were and how you felt when you listened to it, and you realize that that lost moment, well, you *miss it*…"

He smiled.

"It's the first time in your life, and it surprises you. It had never happened to you that a memory was accompanied by heartache…by nostalgia…It's a new thing, and it feels good. You even enjoy it…But you don't know, you can't know that that's exactly the moment when you stop being young…And you don't imagine that there will be other moments like that, a lot of them, and that the heartache you've just felt will very soon stop making you feel good…You don't know, you can't know that you have just fallen into the trap that is the most terrible, the mellowest, and cruelest, and most pitiless of all…the trap of remembering your youth as though it had been full of only wonderful things, while that's not true, damn it, for anybody…It's never true…Because we suffer like dogs, when we're young. I know that well, and I believe you all know that well, too…"

He took a long pause, then whispered:

"It's not the objects I miss, from those years. And you neither…It's something very different…It's much, much more…"

He pulled some sheets of paper out of the back pocket of his jeans, opened them up, and a huge applause broke out. Vezzosi waited there motionless until it died out, then he flashed a smile.

"I think this is the beginning of the new novel…"

The applause started up again, and again Vezzosi waited there, immobile, until it ended. Then, in the total silence, he began to read.

"So, my darling girl, I'm going to tell you this incredible dream I had. It starts with me in bed and I wake up with a start, because I hear banging on my door and a voice tells me that I have to get up right away because it's late, and it's mother's voice, my mother, but not the weak voice she has now; it's that shrill and decisive voice of when she was forty. She opens the door and comes in the room, complains about the stale air, goes to the window, and there's that flapping sound of the blind suddenly rolling up, and the room is bathed in light and I try to open my eyes, but I have to close them again because there's too much light, and meanwhile I hear her leave the room to go wake up my brothers... Because in the dream I have brothers... And then I open my eyes and find myself in my room, in the little bedroom I had when I was sixteen, with the blue wall-to-wall carpet and the light wood wall closet, and the white cabinet full of books, and Dad's Philips stereo with the piles of my records next to it, and the cork panel with the pictures of tennis players hung on it with tacks... It's all there, nothing missing, and when I get out of bed, I realize immediately that it's not a dream like the others, because I can feel the carpet under my feet, that sort of scratchiness, you know, and so I go to the mirror and see that I'm a kid. I'm sixteen, not fifty-four, and I weigh seventy kilos, that is, practically *the half of me* and I get the giggles over how young, and slim, and strong I am...It's as though I were *new*, shit, without the paunch and without the hair on my belly and without the tattoos, and when I run my hands over my body, I can feel that I have abdominals...My abdominals have come back and I don't have an inch of fat, and then my face...I look at myself and I'm a kid, and my heart starts beating as fast as it can...My teeth are milky white, like chalk, my skin fresh, taut as a drum, my forest of hair, curly, raven black, and the way my shoulder blades are sticking out, it looks like they're going to break through my skin...Then I hear my mother calling me from downstairs, because breakfast is ready, and so I go to the closet and open it and there are all my T-shirts, and shirts and jeans...My stuff, my things...I stand there for a bit, looking at them, and I put on the ones I miss the most, the blue UCLA T-shirt and the denim shirt with the mother-of-pearl buttons that I think I still have somewhere, but in the dream, it's new, dark blue, and I slip on my most faded 501s and the Panatta Superga tennis shoes, the white ones with the blue logo, and I start to laugh because it's all so beautiful and new, and it all looks great on me...I scramble down the stairs and am flabbergasted with my mouth hanging open, because my mother is young and pretty again, with her hair pulled back and a flowery dressing gown, and she smokes, while she pours the milk in my cup and says I have to hurry, and I don't answer because I'm afraid my voice would be my voice from now and if I spoke she would realize that I'm not really a young boy of sixteen, and then my brothers come in and they're older and bigger

than I am, two towers that I've never seen before, and they
shout at me that I'd better move, and I'm a vagabond, and I'm
going to end up badly, and I even get a slap on the back of my
head...I follow them out to the garage, where there are three
Vespas all in a line, and they take off and I stay there alone,
looking at the white Primavera, the one that you've driven,
too, my darling girl, only it's brand-new, and it starts on the
first try and makes that irresistible rumbling sound, and I get
on it, put it in first, and take off, too, without a helmet, and
it's beautiful, believe me, the cool air, the sounds, and I start to
laugh again: all I do is laugh, in the dream, and I get into the
traffic and everybody's going fast and blowing their horns, and
straining the gears, and so I strain them too and smell the fantastic odor of two-stroke mix, because in the dream I can also
smell odors, but when I get to school it's late, and everyone's already gone in and so I start running down the empty hallways,
and I struggle to remember which class I'm in. I think it must be
the A, I've always been in A, but is it 3A or 4A? I stop a janitor
who asks me if I'm pulling his chain, but then he accompanies
me to 3A, and when I go into class, the *professoressa* scolds me
for being late and I apologize, and I sit at a desk, and she's at
the blackboard explaining some equations, and I look around
but I don't recognize any of my classmates. I'm surrounded by
a bunch of strangers, and I remain silent because I understand
that the dream will last as long as no one discovers that inside
the young boy, there's me, and then the bell rings for the last
hour and I go back home for lunch, and at table my brothers

aren't there anymore but there's my dad, who is really young, not much older than a boy, he's always serious and never looks at me and doesn't say anything, and I'm really hungry and take a double helping of pasta with tomato sauce that is really delicious, because in the dream I can also taste flavors, and a grilled pork chop with salad dressed with lemon, and when I get up from the table I realize that I'm free, totally free, and I've got nothing to do, and so I get back on the Vespa and start going around town that is the same as it used to be, with the streets running in different directions, and it looks beautiful, just beautiful, and I say hello to everybody, even people I don't know, even people I've never seen, and everybody smiles at me and says hello and says to me: *Ciao, Vittorio, it's so nice that you're back*, and as I'm stopped at a traffic light, I'm flanked by a classmate of mine who died young but in the dream he's still alive, and he has a Vespa like mine, and then I take him aside, and it doesn't matter at all anymore if my voice comes out as an old voice and the dream ends: I have to tell him to be careful going around that curve, where he was hit head-on by a car, and even better to never go there at all, on that road, and when I tell him, my voice is perfect, it's my voice as a kid and I make him promise, and then we go together to our usual bar and we hang out there outside, shooting the shit, and meanwhile all our other friends show up, and then the girls, there are a lot of us, all sitting on our Vespas and Ciaos, and there are so many of us we almost block the street, and everybody goes on and on about what we're going to do tomorrow, and where we're going to go for the summer, and who's going to become what, and everyone wants to go to America, and to London, and Paris, and then I notice that it's almost sundown and I get a chill, because I know that it will all really come to an end at sundown, and I don't want to make the shitty impression, vanishing in front of everybody like a ghost, and so I say good-bye, bid farewell to my companions, I hug them one and all, and go off on my Vespa, and start to climb up the hill that stands above the town, and when I get to that clearing where I used to go to kiss the girls, the sun by then is almost all down behind the mountains, and a ray of light shines through, the last ray, that strikes me right in the eyes and blinds me, and I wake up in my room, this morning, and start to write this story, my darling girl, my love…"

He refolded the papers and put them back in his pocket, then he dried a tear on his cheek. The audience was mute.

"Ciao, take care. I love you. Ciao."

And as the world's biggest applause erupted, Vezzosi turned around and walked off, disappearing instantly into the dark in the back of the stage to reappear immediately in front of us.

"Come on, Zapata! Let's go!" he said, and then grabbed the hand of Milena, who was crying, and exited with long strides the backstage to go down the stairs and make his way into the pavilion with the stands.

After a few seconds of bewilderment, I followed them, my heart in my mouth, short of breath, my vision blurred by emotion.

"This is Allegra, Vezzosi," I said to him, gasping, because to reach him I'd had to run, with her by the hand, pretending to protest about all the hubbub. And he:

"My pleasure, Allegra."

But he didn't even look at her. His eyes were fixed to the front as he made his way through the exhibitors, to the tune of *excuse us, folks, please, excuse us,* and it took no time at all, only a minute, to get through the pavilion, pass through all that bric-a-brac, exit, get into the Jeep, turn on the engine, and peel out, at top speed.

At Malpensa Airport

• • •

IT DIDN'T TAKE us long at all to get to Malpensa, fifteen minutes or so, and during the trip nobody said a word. We left the Jeep in a no-parking zone, Vezzosi took Milena by the hand, and they strode into that empty airport, ten steps in front of me and Allegra.

They chatted for a few seconds in front of the departures screen, then she hugged him and kissed him, and he started jogging toward one of the many ticket counters.

I joined him when he was already joking with the two women at the counter, who had recognized him and apologized for not being able to come to hear him at the fair, and already they were pulling out all the stops and smiling as they explained to him that he was making a great deal, because by buying the tickets this way, at the last minute, *first class cost the same as business.*

He pulled out the Diners card, gave me a wink, rubbed it between his hands, and handed it over to the young admirers, who chirped that it was years since they'd seen a Diners Club card, and after a bit of digitation, handed him two tickets that, as he had expressly requested, were printed on sheets of paper.

"There, that's done," he said as we headed back toward our girlfriends. "Milena, let's go. In a few minutes we have to board...!"

She said good-bye to Allegra with a brief hug, then came toward me and gave me two kisses on the cheek.

"Thanks, Emiliano. Thanks for everything, really."

And I, finally:

"But what's going on? Excuse me, I don't understand. Can somebody explain, please?"

And Allegra:

"They're going to Los Angeles. And then they're going on a trip around the world."

I stared at Vezzosi, my mouth wide open.

"But what...no, come on, excuse me...That is, now? Like this? But you don't even have any bags..."

Milena smiled and shrugged her shoulders.

"We can buy everything there, Zapata. No problem," said Vezzosi.

"And your passports?"

"Those we have," said Vezzosi, and he held out his right hand to Allegra, who squeezed it between both of hers. "Excuse me for before, but it was a difficult moment. I'm very happy to meet you. But wait, do you have gray eyes? What luck...Do me a big favor, take care of this guy, because he is a real thoroughbred. He always talks about you, says you're the woman of his life. Did you see the tattoo he got himself?"

Allegra stared at me, and I stared at Vezzosi.

"Vittorio," Milena said, "you are such an elephant... Now you've ruined everything..."

"Why, was it supposed to be a surprise? I'm sorry, Zapata, oh, what can I say... At this point, you might as well show it to her, come on..."

I obeyed like a robot, and I unbuttoned my shirt to show everybody the name Allegra that I'd had tattooed on my heart, feeling infinitely ashamed because she looked at it without saying a thing.

"Nice," Milena finally said, in the void of that immense empty airport.

I rebuttoned my shirt and said to Vezzosi:

"Now, you tell me, please. What's going on?"

He handed the tickets to Milena and asked her to head toward check-in, then he led me over in front of the glass panel that looked out onto the airport taxiing area, and he started looking at a big Aeroflot plane that was looming over everything all by itself.

"What's going on is I'm taking her away with me, Zapata... Now that I've found her again, I want to be with her, I want to live with her... I want to watch her while she sleeps, say good morning to her every day, buy her clothes and eyeglasses... I want to cook for her, I want to massage her feet every night, on the couch, while we're watching a movie that we've already seen many times...And then I want to listen to music with her, lie out in the sun with her...I want to have her drink the best wines in the world, and make her laugh, and be quiet and listen to her talk, understand? But I can't do that in Florence...No, we've got to leave, go far away, change everything, erase everything and start from scratch, without the past...Enough of the past! I can't stand the fucking past anymore..."

Then he turned to look at me.

"Because it's over, Zapata. You heard my male and female readers applauding Casamonti, didn't you?"

"What? What's over?"

"Everything." He smiled and opened up his arms. "Everything we were and knew. The West. I think. Its whole canon."

"I don't understand, Vezzosi."

"One day, you will. When these shithead demagogues take away those three or four little things that you now take for granted...You know, democracy, progress, people's right to live as they please, science, merit, solidarity for the hopeless. Then you'll understand..."

All of a sudden, he seemed tired. He stopped. Took a deep breath, let it out slowly.

"But I don't want to see it, this thing, and so I'll do like the elves, and go off by myself."

He rummaged in his pocket.

"Here are the keys to the car. The house is open. You take care of everything, please."

He held them out to me and I took them. Then he gave me a roll of banknotes.

"You'll need two full tanks, to make it to Florence. Heads up, the coke is in the glove compartment of the Jeep, and in the house there's more in my room. Oh, I was joking when I said it was stuff for retirees... Be careful, Zapata, it's the best, Tony Montana's snow... I told you it was just a little something to make you calm down, and in fact you did calm down, because anyway it's always mind over matter, not vice versa. The body serves to give us pleasure, as long as it lasts, and then so long... Well, I'm off... For anything you need, in any case, you have my phone number..."

"No, actually I don't."

"Really?"

"We've never called each other, you and I."

"Right. You're right. Here it is."

He held the bill from the hotel up against the glass and wrote down on the back a number full of sevens.

"So, talk to you soon, Zapata..."

He held out his arms to hug me.

"No, wait... Wait a minute, please. Was this all planned? Even Milena, I mean?... Everyone knew about it but me?"

"No." He smiled. "What plan... Do I seem to you like someone who plans things? Plus, you were there, too, no? We went straight ahead and let it all hang out, without stopping, ever, it's been fantastic... Nobody who hit the brakes, who broke our balls... You've been great, Zapata, really, you've never held anything back...Oh, we did some incredible things, we were Led Zeppelin...Come on, walk with me..."

I had a thousand things to tell him, but they kept banging into each other in my head, and not even one of them managed to make it out. We headed toward the first-class check-in counter, where Milena and Allegra were chatting with three young women. We only had about fifty meters to go, but his breathing was already accelerating and he had slowed his pace. In an instant, everything had changed.

"Everything okay, Vezzosi?"

"Hmm. All told...I'm not so sure...Not great...Maybe I'm a little nervous...You know, check-in for me has always been pretty tough, I don't know why, really...Doesn't it bother you?"

He stopped, his eyes fixed on the ground. He was gasping.

"Come on, Vezzosi...This time, you've got to do it, that's all there is to it."

"So, he told you, eh, that troublemaker of an African..."

He took a long deep breath, as though he were starving for air, then he closed his eyes.

"You want to stop in the bathroom for a minute?"

"No, no...Bathroom for what..."

Milena turned around and came toward us. She seemed worried.

"Will you give me your passport, Vittorio? They're already boarding..."

He rummaged in his jacket and held it out to her.

"Are you coming?"

"Just a minute, love...I'll come in a minute, don't worry."

Milena seemed as though she was on the verge of saying something, then she turned and went back to the check-in counter. Vezzosi's eyes were shiny, as though he were running a fever.

"Help me, Zapata, otherwise I won't be able to do it...It won't take much, just got to break the moment...A little like last night..."

He put a hand on my shoulder.

"Say something to me, come on...Piss me off...Nobody is better at that than you...But nothing about Milena, this time, eh..."

He tried to smile, but his forehead was beaded with sweat. It was about to happen.

It was true. He was shutting down...

"N-now, Zapata, now, c-c-come on..."

"There's one question I do have..."

"Yeah? And wh-what? Tell-tell—me ri-right away..."

"It's not one, Vezzosi. There are two. The first one is this...Even if in some way you managed to get on this airplane, how the hell will you be able to make it back from Los Angeles? Because I won't be there, and neither will Mamadou, and I just can't see your Milena acting as your caregiver..."

"Ca-care-gi-giver? What the fuck are you talking about?"

"That's exactly what I mean. *Caregiver* is the right word. You're not a self-sufficient person, Vezzosi. In fact, I'm going to go tell her that right now..."

He squeezed my arm hard.

"Do-don't pull any bullshit, kiddo..." he growled.

"And then there's the second question...Excuse me, *Maestro*, but if the West is finished and there's no saving anybody and the past can't come back because trying to make it come back didn't work for Gatsby, you and she, where the fuck are you going, eh, at fifty-five years old?"

He wrinkled his eyebrows and I got ready for the slap in the face, but his face looked like it was melting, and finally he smiled.

"Man, Mamadou sure had your number...You really are an arrogant punk and a son of a bitch..."

"Thank you, *Maestro*."

"But I feel better already..."

"See?"

He breathed in deep, and exhaled.

"Yes, I feel much better, really. I'm going. This time I'm going. Thanks, Zapata."

"Signor Vezzosi and Signora Zucchi are expected at gate A01 for immediate boarding."

Milena was coming toward us. We only had a few seconds.

"Oh, aren't you even going to answer me? Oh, why don't you ever answer me?"

He smiled. He was himself again.

"You're something when you're pissed off, Zapata, but now excuse me. I've got a plane to catch, and if I catch this one, then I'll catch them all...And about Gatsby...Oh, Gatsby didn't know a damn thing about life...After all, he was just a guy from Minnesota..."

He shrugged his shoulders.

"What can I tell you, Zapata, I'm going to give it a whirl. We'll see how it goes..."

He gave me a big hug.

"Thank you. Thanks a million for everything."

And while that bear was squeezing me, I realized I was about to collapse, worse than him. I was sure I would never see him again, and something shut my throat. I whispered in his ear.

"But me, Vezzosi...what am I supposed to do with my life?"

He released from the hug, he grabbed me by my meager biceps.

"Don't let them see you crying, buddy."

He launched a brief glance at Milena, to implore her to stop. Then he looked me in the eye and whispered:

"You have to save the world, Zapata."

"Me? And how do I do that?"

"What questions...Like it's always been done. You write a novel."

Then he turned, took Milena under his arm, and they disappeared beyond the security checkpoint.

Blessed Clara

. . .

BEFORE GETTING ON the road for Florence, Allegra made me pull up the windshield on the Jeep and put the top back in place.

"But where the fuck are the doors?" she complained and, while we were stopped to fill up, she announced in rapid succession that Vezzosi was a genius and Milena was gorgeous, but between them it would never work out; that without a beard I looked worse, and seemed like some kind of bubble-head; that tattoos were for football players and she didn't like them and mine I should immediately get removed by laser; that the *prehistoric* music on the cassette I had put in the stereo, the one with the label NELLO IL GIOVANE aka NEIL YOUNG, was virtually unlistenable.

After some fruitless attempts to get the radio to work— *You mean, sorry, but the only way to change the station is this knob?*—she said she was exhausted, ordered me to go as slow as I could, curled up in the seat, and fell asleep, not to wake up until we were just about at the gates of Florence.

My phone vibrated constantly for the whole trip, but I didn't look at it even once. When we got to Bologna, I stopped to fill it up again, and I felt like snorting a little coke, but I was afraid she'd wake up, and then without Vezzosi, it wouldn't have been the same, so I headed straight for the panoramic route.

When I dropped her off in front of her front door, Allegra went into the house all groggy, without even a kiss or a hug, blaming me for making her come down with a cold *with all that fucking wind*, and then a fatigue came over me that was terrible, mortal, enough to make me stop right there and sleep in the car, but I forced myself to go as far as Vezzosi's house, to leave the Jeep there and take back my scooter.

When I got there, the gas tank was on empty. Vezzosi was right: even going slow, two fill-ups were barely enough to make it back from Milan, for the last great American carburetor engine. There was a beautiful sunset, from up there on those desolate hills, and for the first time that bulky box of a house looked good to me, with the bare stone all lit up in pink and yellow.

The door was open and I went in. The silence was total. The house was as clean as an operating room, completely in order, the refrigerator full. I went upstairs, and the first of the two doors opened onto a large, nearly empty white room, its wooden floor polished to a sheen, wall closets and a terrace looking out on the woods below. There was an unmade bed and a glass bed table hosting a lamp and a book by Sebald, nothing else.

Only when I sat down on the bed did I notice the brown truck canvas hanging on the wall. It was almost completely covered with a script, BLESSED CLARA, written in white paint. I looked at it for a while. Maybe it was a painting. My eyes were closing and I lay down. When the writing started to blur, I fell asleep.

I woke up at dawn with the sunlight invading the room, and I went to open the second door. It opened onto a large room, illuminated by a glass wall with a view of Florence, and chaos reigned.

He had framed everything, Vezzosi, and filled the walls with quadrangles, large and small. There was a poster of the 1939 New York World's Fair, a picture of him with a Ferrari cap together with Michael Schumacher and Montezemolo, various handwritten sheets of paper that appeared to be letters that I promised myself I would look at with greater attention, two yellowed pages of the *New York Times* with a review of *The Wolves Inside*, a restaurant bill for two thousand euros, a medical report declaring that Vezzosi Vittorio, born in Florence on 11/19/1964, had been subjected to electroshock therapy.

And then books, here too, books everywhere, of every dimension and subject, almost all illustrated with photos. Many were on gardening, piled next to and above and under monographs by artists totally unknown to me and dozens of volumes on subjects so incongruous among them that they seemed to have been collected by different people: boxing, the art of wrought iron, space exploration, white arms, white wines, jewels, drugs, Jacquard weaving, motorcycles, bridges, wood and glass houses in California, stereos, the Apuan Alps, jet planes, Ferrari. And all kinds of manuals: on interrogation techniques of the American police, on gazpacho, on how to write television screenplays, on stock market investing, on glass blowing, on the occult arts.

Dozens of biographies, almost all of them in English, of famous writers and other celebrities whose names I'd never heard but who must have been famous, at one time: stylists, directors, producers, porno stars, artists, entrepreneurs, astronauts. Dozens of framed photographs of the same girl, portrayed from the crib to graduation. An incredibly slim horn, two meters long, all contorted and yellowed, mounted on a marble base. A white bear skin rolled up in a corner. Two old trunks all scratched up. The headboard of a bed. A metallic apparatus with glass valves and a gothic script that said "McIntosh MC60." Plaques of literary prizes in various languages. A dozen small and very small trophies from tennis tournaments that went from 1976 to 1979. A small model of the Concorde. A piece of wood painted white with the script BEST OF TIMES. An Olivetti typewriter with a Hebrew keyboard. One of those clocks with rotating numbers like the ones on departures/arrivals boards in airports from a thousand years ago, that flipped and spun but showed the wrong time. Two small paintings, one in a blue that seemed to pulsate and the other red with just a date in the center. Garden scissors. A spray can of WD-40. A big knife with a curved blade. An American flag carefully folded like the ones that in movies they give to the parents of soldiers killed in war. A dozen wooden tennis rackets. Two boxing gloves. Five bottles of Caol Iola whisky, all half-empty, all greater than 60 proof. An hourglass a half meter tall with white sand inside. A small glass display case half-full of some black grainy substance, with a label written by hand: LAVA FROM AETNA. A glass-doored cabinet with four pistols, one antique, a derringer, with an ivory handle, and three rifles, one a pump-action. In one corner, half-covered by a white sheet, the end piece of a metal pipe that must have been a bazooka. A picture of an enormous, smiling Black man, in a white jacket and open shirt showing his chest, his forehead beaded with drops of sweat, with the dedication: *To the Beautiful, Beautiful Arianna, Barry White*. A small, marvelous Mercator projection. A silver sugar bowl that, once the top was removed, turned out to be full of cocaine.

And in the center of the room there was a table, and on the table, there was a computer, a desktop, turned on. I moved the mouse and text appeared on the screen. I went to the sugar bowl, stuck my finger into the cocaine, tapped it on the table, created without hurrying two large lines with an old Blockbuster card in the name of Mamadou Diallo that was nearby, and snorted the lines. Then I sat down, and started to read:

> *My adored darling girl,*
> *Excuse me for not managing to come to London this time as well: I'm a total disaster as a father. It made me*

feel very badly, I really thought I could make it, but instead no. I'm making some progress, though, it seems, and this time I almost pulled it off. The next time, I'll make it for sure, I promise you.

These are strange days, and I find myself constantly drinking tonic water with Tanqueray and listening over and over to old sad songs, as you call them, "Don't Cry" by Guns N' Roses most of all and above all, with its perfect high-school kid lyric whined by Axl at his best, and imbued with the filthy solemnity of old Slash's solo.

Listen to it, please, it's a song that wants to recount the farewell of two kids—nothing special, to be sure—but it seems to me it succeeds rather perfectly in recounting a farewell, maybe every farewell, even ours, the ones between me and you, that cost me more and more, and that I try in vain to wrap in a gauze of tenderness, but they're hard as stone, and sharp and gray and icy and brusque, and every time I think about them I want to cry because I'm as soft as a sponge these days, and I don't even know why I'm telling you these things. Maybe I shouldn't, no, I'm sure I shouldn't, but I feel the need to be sincere, for once, and so I'm unloading on you all of this sappy stuff. I hope it's not too unpleasant for you. Be patient. Put up with me. I know that I'm sentimental and intrusive, and that this is not the right way to act, but when the time comes we're all sentimental and intrusive, me first of all.

These are strange days, like I said, and the nights are the worst, spent looking at the shadows that chase one another across the ceiling and remembering my life that seems like it's gone by in a flash, by God; thinking about all the good I didn't do when I was able to and it would have taken so little, almost nothing; of all the people I've disappointed and should not have disappointed, including you, my little one; of all the promises I didn't keep, and all the future that should have been and wasn't, and so on and so on...Ah, if I could switch it off, my mind, or rather my memory, this bastard that never stays quiet and always reprimands me!

I've been thinking that I could give up once and for all, on that disastrous novel "on tragedies and miseries," as you say, and start right away on a new one. Fresh, intriguing, short, rapid, concentrated. A love story, maybe. What do you say? You think it could work?

Not too long ago some ideas came to me that actually seemed pretty nice. A glimmer of a plot, finally, all of a sudden, and I found myself jotting down notes again in the middle of the night, leaning into the dim light of the bedside table lamp, half blind because my glasses had been left in the other room and I didn't feel like getting out of bed, and I tried to write as well as possible in the fog that was looming before my eyes, and since I didn't have a notebook I wrote on the blank pages at the end of a book by Sebald, On the Natural History of Destruction, *because I'm rereading Sebald, always need to reread Sebald, and in the end I filled two pages with notes, practically blind, and I made myself write as well as possible, not only the concepts but also the words because otherwise I can't reread what I wrote, and when I finished I fell asleep satisfied, finally calm, the pen still in my hand, and luckily, while I was sleeping I didn't stick it in my eye, because the next morning I found a lot of doodles on the sheets.*

Then, though, when I tried to reread it, I realized it was just a bunch of bullshit. Nothing but nighttime thoughts, those minuscule and mediocre ghosts that have no body, nor life, nor meaning, but come running as soon as you turn out the light, and start gnawing away at your soul, and that you can never manage to get rid of: recriminations, spiteful comments, memories of suffered wrongs, fears, lost opportunities, failed vendettas, mistakes, millions of mistakes, and then rage, a sea of rage, and me drowning in it…

I threw it all away and I went back to reread a wonderful book by Oriana Fallaci. I know that you have problems with her because of those things on Islam, but this book is one you have to read right away, please.

It's called That Day on the Moon *and it recounts the Apollo 11 mission, and she is so full of passion and enthusiasm and competence and bravura! You can tell she believes every word she's writing, and she knows everything.*

She is totally informed, Oriana, she doesn't just go there and do the number of those reporters who just tell us the things as they see them, but since they don't know anything about what they're seeing, they don't understand a damn thing, and get lost and end up telling us about themselves, of how much they're suffering for lack of love, about their father and mother, their dog, how much they drink, and they get by on that, while the story they were supposed to tell goes down the drain.

No, she explains in minute detail all the technical problems that NASA had to overcome to get to launch day, the procedure for landing on the moon, how the LEM module is designed: she tells us of all the dangers of contamination... She explains things to her readers, you see what I'm saying? She doesn't just recount things, she explains them to us. And there's a sea, no, an ocean, between recounting and explaining...

She knows she has the good fortune to witness one of the most fundamental events in history, and she has prepared for it. She studied for a long time to be the best possible witness of the moment that changed the world forever. Because she, Fallaci, was there, right there, at the center of everything, at Cape Canaveral, to see with her own eyes the liftoff of the Saturn rocket on top of which was perched the capsule with the astronauts, and after the launch she got on an airplane and flew out to Houston, to the Control Center, to follow the entire mission.

She had met the astronauts, you know? Neil Armstrong and Buzz Aldrin and Michael Collins, and a lot of others. She had interviewed them a bunch of times. She says that, after all, they were middle-class guys from the heartland and they didn't feel all that emotional about being part of that immense undertaking. They were soldiers and they had a mission and they had to see it through, that's all. A normal technological accomplishment, they said. Can you imagine? She lived in a world, where going to the moon could be considered a normal technological accomplishment, because in the meantime there were already preparations to go to Mars, and that, yes, was going to be hard…

At the end of the book there is a marvelous piece, where Fallaci transcribes the whole telephone call that she made to the editorial board of Europeo—*at the time a famous weekly magazine*—*during the moments of the launch, and she explains that Jules Verne had already described that mission a century before, and his spaceship also took off from Florida, in summer, and held three men, and then she says that it would have taken Homer to recount that giant step for mankind, someone much greater than she! And when the Saturn's engines start up and the countdown begins, her voice cracks and she confesses to having cried while recounting a blast of air that "almost knocked us to the ground," and a thunderous roar that "sounds like a bombardment, but doesn't kill anybody."*

That's what she says about the rocket on liftoff, I want to write it out for you exactly, word for word: "Oh, what a stupendous thing… it's rising so slowly, you know, so slowly… it's going to the moon… the moon… I wish that nobody would die today…"

How much I would have liked to have known her! Because I was alive when they walked on the moon. I was five years old, and that July night, Daddy took me in his arms and he showed me the moon shining bright between the branches of the big magnolia tree that filled the garden of the house they had rented for the summer at Vittoria Apuana—They're funny, big trees in small gardens, aren't they? Do you like them? I do, yes, a lot!—and he told me that there were some men, up there. I remember everything, as though it were right now. That cold light, that immense thought, the sensation of being in some way already on my way to the moon because in my father's arms I was already a meter and a half above ground, and above all the certainty that I would get there, too, one day, to the moon…

I went to the bookstore and bought it for you, That Day on the Moon, and then I went to DHL to get it to you as soon as possible "express," as we used to say. And while I was in line to pay, with the book in hand, a jerk behind me saw the cover and said: "Too bad the whole thing was made up. They never went to the moon." I turned around, and I was about to punch him out. Really, one second more and that would have been it. Then, though, I saw that he was little more than a teenager, and he had that bleary-eyed, surly face of the repressed, of the know-nothings who are happy to be ignorant, of the dullards, of those who do nothing their whole lives but envy others, and so I laughed in his face.

Oh, I hate these buttheads so much, these imbeciles who don't believe in anything and don't know anything and yet they're convinced they know everything, and they've created a global tribunal of nitwits and every day they sit there at their computers and decide what's true and what's not, who's pure and who's not. Well, I am not pure! I commit their sins every day, and I violate their miserable laws every day!

I hate them, damn it, these dimwit wackoffs with their fingers pointed, who want to rewrite history and pass judgment on the dead and impose their morality on artists and try to censor the works of geniuses and decide which books it's okay to read and which paintings to admire, what films to watch and what songs to listen to. Damn them, let the wind disperse them like farts!

Anyway, I sent you the book, my darling girl, and it'll be there faster than you can say the name. Read it as soon as you can, so we can talk about it, because I've always really liked talking to you, ever since you were little, and you explained to me the stories of the cartoons, and every time it took you at least half an hour because you wanted to

explain them to me "really good," remember? And when I
took you to London to see the changing of the guard and
you just had to have a bearskin cap like the ones the sol-
diers wore? Hey, do you remember?

The days are hot, very hot, but in the evening, it cools
down, luckily, and yesterday you could see Florence per-
fectly, and so I got the idea to do that thing of ours to
take Under the Volcano *and open it at random. Oh, it's*
incredible. This time, too, I happened on a gem that I'd
missed or had forgotten! It's something that Señora Gre-
gorio says to the Consul, listen:

I have no house, only a shadow,
But whenever you are in need
Of a shadow, my shadow is yours

Not bad, eh? It would be a great tattoo, "My shadow is
yours," no? What do you say? For me it brightened a bad
day, maybe the worst day of all.

I hadn't done anything all day except rack my brain
about how miserable my life would have been without
the novels and stories and the poetry of those writers
who have distilled the pain of their lives and offered it to
us without asking anything in return, if not a little loose
change and the desire and the time to read.

But for a lot of them it wasn't enough to lock it up inside
their books, all that pain, to free themselves of it. It kept on

coming out, grabbing hold of them, especially at night, I think. There are a lot of them who didn't make it through, you know? More men than women, who knows why?

I kept on imagining them in their last days, walking around the house with their heads down, alone, defeated, invaded by the void, unkempt, mute, badly dressed, their eyes emptied out, their thinking debilitated, their every word withered, all sense of the future erased…

Hunter Thompson put a pistol to his head at age sixty-seven, sitting at his typewriter, in his home, near Aspen, Colorado.

Hemingway killed himself at sixty-one, his mind and memory ruined by electroshock, with a rifle shot to the head, in Ketchum, a small town in the middle of nowhere, I think it's in Idaho.

Paul Celan threw himself into the Seine one night in April, at fifty, and you must know that in 1991, long before I started writing my book, I accompanied Fede on a business trip to newly liberated Berlin and we went to see the big Kiefer exhibition at the Nationalgalerie, and on a lot of those gigantic paintings on the Shoah there was written in charcoal Dein aschenes Haar Sulamith, "Your black hair Sulamith," and Dein goldenes Haar Margarete, "Your golden hair Margarete," and if Sulamith's hair was nests of human hair coming out of rusted lead plates, Margarete's hair was strips of dried straw that seemed to have been strewn by the wind onto those enormous canvases, and when we read in

*the catalogue of the exhibition that they were verses of
Paul Celan, we rushed to buy one of his books, and I
recited his poems in the car and Fede tried to translate
them, relying on the fifty words of his textile German
that he knew while Thomas, his titanic agent, drove silently toward the grand Berlinese cathedrals of clothing,
all bankrupt today despite the formidable names they
bore: Hommel & Klatt, Hensel & Mortensen, Umlauf
& Klein, Wilhelm Krause…*

*Petronius wished to die as he had lived, lightheartedly,
during one of his banquets, in Cuma, near Naples. He
was thirty-nine. Tacitus says that "having made an inci-
sion in his veins and then, according to his humor, bound
them up, he again opened them, while he conversed with
his friends, not in a serious strain or on topics that might
win for him the glory of courage. And he listened to them
as they repeated, not thoughts on the immortality of the
soul or on the theories of philosophers, but light poetry
and playful verses."*

*Cesare Pavese killed himself at forty-one with packets
of sleeping powder, in Turin, in the cruel days of the end
of August. When he was eighteen, overwhelmed by the
suicide of a classmate, he had written:*

I went one evening in December
along a narrow country road
completely deserted, with tumult in my heart
with me, I had a revolver

Sylvia Plath was with her little children in London, in an apartment that she had rented in the building where Yeats had lived, and one night, at age thirty, she stuffed every opening in the kitchen with sheets and towels, stuck her head in the oven, and turned on the gas, in a suicide that must have inspired the one of James Incandenza... You'll remember that, the character in Infinite Jest who shoots those totally crazy and ingenious avant-garde films, and one day he drills a hole in the glass of the microwave oven, sticks his head in, seals shut all the openings with aluminum foil, and then turns on the oven, and when his son Hal comes back home after tennis practice, exhausted and famished, as he's taking off his shoes in the entryway, just before going in the kitchen to see his father with his head sticking inside what's left of the microwave oven, he thinks, "Something smells really nice in the house."

Salgari killed himself in a rage against his publishers who had always exploited him. He cut his throat with a razor, at age forty, at dawn, in a gulley in the middle of the woods, not far from his home in Turin.

Sándor Márai committed suicide in San Diego, California, at eighty-eight, with a pistol shot, after the death of his companion.

Von Kleist shot himself at thirty-four, together with a gravely ill female friend, in Berlin, on the shore of a lake.

Robert E. Howard, the author of Conan the Barbarian, also shot himself in the temple, at thirty, in the

*parking lot of a Texas hospital, when he learned that his
adored mother would never regain consciousness.*

*At fifty-nine, Virginia Woolf filled the pockets of her
overcoat with rocks and jumped into the Ouse River, in
Sussex, England.*

*Franco Lucentini threw himself down the stairwell of
his building, at eighty-one, in Turin, and perhaps Levi
did the same thing, my great, poor Primo Levi.*

*And David Foster Wallace hanged himself in a garage
at forty-six, in Claremont, which is one of the most beautiful towns in California, in the immense Los Angeles
County. I've been there.*

*Now I'll leave you—strictly in the metaphorical
sense, certainly—and try to go to sleep. I apologize for
the length of this letter, but I don't feel like correcting it.
Rereading it, it seems disjointed and rambling, but you'll
understand everything, I'm sure. And anyway, pardon
me, I didn't want to bore you, much less worry you.*

*Please know that I'm well, very well, and waiting for
you here at your house, when your studies allow. I entrust
myself to you, my darling girl, and I embrace you with all
my strength.*

Honor your true self, as always.

Your Daddy

There was nothing else in the computer. No documents,
no archive. The operating system, Word, a copy of Outlook

chock full of emails between him and his daughter, and that's it.

"Son of a bitch," I whispered into the empty air, and smiled.

I set down on the table the anthology of Epictetus, shot a last glance at the sugar bowl full of cocaine, went out of the house, got on the scooter, and went on my way, down the mule path.

Every Now and Again

. . .

EVERY NOW AND again, I go back there, to Vezzosi's house.

I take care of it.

I act as a sort of custodian, make sure everything is in place, that nobody goes in. Sometimes I also stay overnight. It's cooler than in Florence, and then, it has air-conditioning.

I hang out there, think, go for walks. Water the plants. Contemplate the vertical drop of my followers on Instagram. Send away the journalists and the other supplicants. I drink his wine, read his books, watch his movies, listen to his music. Every now and again I snort some of his cocaine. I've learned how to drive his Vespas, and I've also gone back to get the doors to the Jeep in Frosini's palm grove.

His book, however, I have yet to open.

And I haven't heard from him.

Nobody has heard from him, not even his daughter, but Milena continues to post on Instagram pictures of deserted beaches, stray dogs, pages from the *Volcano*, sunsets, tropical flowers, and empty bottles of wine, so I'm not worried.

Everything's fine, I think.

This morning, on waking up, I remembered something he said to me while we were driving on the panoramic route to Bologna. In the middle of all that wind, I couldn't understand half of what he said, but he was shouting about a scene in a Fellini movie that I absolutely had to see, otherwise I would never accomplish anything in life.

"It's in *La Dolce Vita*. It concerns Marcello and a glass of milk."

At one point, in the middle of the night, Anita Ekberg picks up a stray cat and asks Mastroianni to find some milk for it. He protests: *But, honey, where can I find milk at this hour?*, but anyway he runs off to look for some while she wanders around Rome with the kitten on her head and is astounded on seeing the marvel of the Fountain of Trevi, and then, after she's started walking in the fountain as if it were hers—because, actually, it *is* hers—Marcello reappears, beautiful as a ray of sunshine, with a glass of milk on a plate, and I don't know if I understood it the way Vezzosi understood it, this thing, maybe not, but my thought was that all of cinema is in there, in that glass of milk that arrives out of nowhere.

But not only all of cinema.

All of our stories, too.

And even life.

I mean, if a woman asks you to, you have got to find a glass of milk, in the middle of the night, in a deserted city.

It's all there.

Acknowledgments

•   •   •

I must thank Leonardo Bononcini, Chiara Valerio, Teresa Ciabatti, Mario Desiati, Edoardo Rialti, Antonio Sangermano, Quintino Freite, Andrea Salerno, Aldo Niccoli, Michele Pellegrini, Francesco De Vito, Laura Paolucci, Fabio Genovesi, Carmine Schiavo, Sandro Veronesi, Riccardo Gori, Carlo Bardazzi, Flora Leoni, Giuseppe Carmagnini, Paolo Bartolozzi, Emiliano Citarella, Angiolo Barni.

And Ugo Marchetti, my precious and irreplaceable friend who has always made my books better with intrigues, support, validation, and things to be explained house by house.

And then, naturally, Elisabetta, Eugenio, Ettore, Angelica, and my Carlotta.

this is your eternal life